Stanislaw Lem was born on 12 September 1921 in Lvov, Poland (now part of the Soviet Union), and lives with his family in Krakow. Originally trained in medicine he began to write seriously in the 1940's and is now one of Europe's most prolific and articulate writers, as well as being the co-founder of the Polish Astronautical Society and a member of the Polish Cybernetics Association. His books, translated into almost thirty languages, range from novels, which include *The Cyberiad* and *The Investigation*, and screenplays to parody, philosophy and literary criticism. In 1973 he was awarded for his literary achievements the Nebula Award, the highest honour granted by the Polish Ministry of Culture.

Also by Stanislaw Lem

*The Cyberiad*

Stanislaw Lem

# The Futurological Congress

(from the memoirs of Ijon Tichy)

Translated from the Polish
by Michael Kandel

Futura Publications Limited
An Orbit Book

An Orbit Book

First published in Great Britain in 1975
by Martin Secker & Warburg Limited

First Futura Publications edition 1977

Originally published in Polish under the title
*Ze wspomnień Ijona Tichego. Kongres
Futurologiczny in Bezsenność* and by
Wydawnictwo Literackie, Kraków 1971

ISBN 0 8600 7928 7
Printed in Great Britain by
Richard Clay (The Chaucer Press) Ltd,
Bungay, Suffolk

Futura Publications Limited
110 Warner Road, Camberwell
London SE5

# THE FUTUROLOGICAL CONGRESS

**T**HE EIGHTH WORLD FUTUROLOGICAL CONGRESS was held in Costa Rica. To tell the truth, I never would have gone to Nounas if it hadn't been for Professor Tarantoga, who gave me clearly to understand that this was expected of me. He also said —pointedly—that space travel nowadays was an escape from the problems of Earth. That is, one took off for the stars in the hope that the worst would happen and be done with in one's absence. And indeed I couldn't deny that more than once I had peered anxiously out the porthole—especially when returning from a long voyage—to see whether or not our planet resembled a burnt potato. So I didn't argue the point with Tarantoga, but only remarked that, really, I wasn't much of an expert on futurology. His reply was that hardly anyone knows a thing about pumping, and yet we don't stand idly by when we hear the cry of "Man the pumps!"

The directors of the Futurological Association had chosen Costa Rica to be the site of their annual meeting, which this year was to deal exclusively with the population explosion and possible methods of keeping it in check. Costa Rica presently boasts the highest rate of demographic growth in the world; presumably the force of that reality alone was to help spur our deliberations to some successful conclusion. Though there were cynics who observed that only the new Hilton in Nounas had vacancies enough to accommodate all the futurologists, not to mention twice again as many reporters. Inasmuch as this hotel was completely demolished in the course of our conference, I can't be accused of making a plug when I say that the place was absolutely first-rate. These words have particular weight, coming from a confirmed sybarite; for indeed, it was only a sense of duty that had driven me to forsake the comforts of home for the travail of outer space.

The Costa Rica Hilton soared one hundred and six floors upward from its flat, four-story base. On the roof of this lower structure were tennis courts, swimming pools, solariums, racetracks, merry-go-rounds (which simultaneously served as roulette wheels), and shooting galleries where you could fire at absolutely anyone you liked—in effigy—provided you put in your order twenty-four hours in advance, and there were concert amphitheaters equipped with tear gas sprinklers in case the audience got out of hand. I was given a room on the hundredth floor; from it I could see only the top of the bluish brown cloud of smog that coiled about the city. Some of the hotel furnishings puzzled me—the ten-foot crowbar propped up in a corner of the jade and jasper bathroom, for example, or the khaki camouflage cape in the closet, or the sack of hardtack under the bed. Over the tub, next to the towels, hung an enormous spool of standard Alpine rope, and on the door was a card which I first noticed when I went to triple-lock the super-yale. It read: "This Room Guaranteed BOMB-FREE. From the Management."

It is common knowledge that there are two kinds of scholar these days: the stationary and the peripatetic. The stationaries pursue their studies in the traditional way, while their restless colleagues participate in every sort of international seminar and symposium imaginable. The scholar of this second type may be readily identified: in his lapel he wears a card bearing his name, rank and home university, in his pocket sticks a flight schedule of arrivals and departures, and the buckle on

2

his belt—as well as the snaps on his briefcase—are plastic, never metal, so as not to trigger unnecessarily the alarms of the airport scanners that search boarding passengers for weapons. Our peripatetic scholar keeps up with the literature of his field by studying in buses, waiting rooms, planes and hotel bars. Since I was—naturally enough—unacquainted with many of the recent customs of Earth, I set off alarms in the airports of Bangkok, Athens and Costa Rica itself, having six amalgam fillings in my mouth. These I was planning to replace with porcelain in Nounas, but the events that followed so unexpectedly made that quite impossible. As for the Alpine rope, the crowbar, the hardtack and the camouflage cape, one of the members of the American delegation of futurologists patiently explained to me that today's hotels take safety precautions unknown in earlier times. Each of the above items, when included in the room, significantly increases the life expectancy of the occupant. How foolish it was of me, not to have taken those words more seriously!

The sessions were scheduled to begin in the afternoon of the first day, and that morning we all received complete programs of the conference; the materials were handsomely printed up, elegantly bound, with numerous charts and illustrations. I was particularly intrigued by a booklet of embossed sky-blue coupons, each stamped: "Good for One Intercourse."

Present-day scientific conventions, obviously, also suffer from the population explosion. Since the number of futurologists grows in proportion to the increase in magnitude of all humanity, their meetings are marked by crowds and confusion. The oral presentation of papers is quite out of the question; these have to be read in advance. Though there wasn't time for reading anything that morning—the Management treated us all to free drinks. This little ceremony took place without incident, barring the fact that a few rotten tomatoes were thrown at the United States contingent. I was sipping my Martini when I learned from Jim Stantor, a well-known UPI reporter, that a consul and a grade-three attaché of the American Embassy in Costa Rica had been kidnapped at dawn. The abductors were demanding the release of all political prisoners in exchange for the diplomats. To show they meant business, these extremists had already delivered individual teeth of their hostages to the Embassy and various government offices, promising an anatomical escalation. Still, this contretemps did not mar the cordial atmosphere of our morning get-together. The United States ambassador himself was there, and gave a short speech on the need for international cooperation—short, as he was surrounded by six muscular plainclothesmen who kept their guns trained on us all the time. I was rather disconcerted by this, especially when the dark-skinned delegate from India standing next to me had to wipe his nose and reached for the handkerchief in his back pocket. The official spokesman for the Futurological Association assured me afterwards that the measures taken had been both necessary and humane. Bodyguards now employ weapons of high caliber and low penetration, the kind security agents carry on board passenger flights in order that innocent bystanders not be harmed. In the old days it often happened that the bullet which felled the would-be assassin would subsequently pass through five or even six persons who, though minding their own business,

4

were standing directly behind him. Still, the sight of a man at your side crumpling to the floor under heavy fire is not among the most pleasant, even if it *is* the result of a simple misunderstanding, which ends with an exchange of diplomatic notes and official apologies.

But rather than attempt to settle the thorny question of humanitarian ballistics, perhaps I ought to explain why I was unable, all that day, to familiarize myself with the conference materials. So then, after hurriedly changing my blood-spattered shirt, I went to the hotel bar for breakfast, which usually I do not do. My custom is to eat a soft-boiled egg in the morning, but the hotel hasn't yet been built where you can have one sent up to your room that isn't revoltingly cold. This is due, no doubt, to the continually expanding size of metropolitan hotels. If a mile and a half separates the kitchen from your room, nothing will keep that yolk warm. As far as I know, the Hilton experts did study the problem; they came to the conclusion that the only solution would be special dumbwaiters moving at supersonic speeds, but obviously sonic booms in an enclosed area would burst everyone's eardrums. Of course you could always have the automatic cook send the eggs up raw and the automatic bellhop soft-boil them right in your room, except that that would eventually lead to people coming in and out with their own chicken coops. And thus I headed for the bar.

More than ninety-five percent of a hotel's guests are there for some conference or convention. The individual tourist, the single guest without a card in his lapel and briefcase stuffed with programs and memoranda, is as rare as a pearl in the desert. Besides our own group in Costa Rica, there was the Plenary Council of Student Protest Veterans, the Convention of Publishers of Liberated Literature, and the Phillumenist Society (matchbook collectors). As a rule, members of an organization are given rooms on the same floor, but the Management, apparently wishing to honor me, offered me one on the hundredth. It had its own palm tree grove, in which an all-girl orchestra played Bach while performing a cleverly choreographed striptease. I could have done quite well without all this, but unfortunately there were no other vacancies, so I was obliged to stay where they put me. Scarcely had I taken a seat at the bar on my floor when a broad-shouldered individual with a jet-black beard (a beard that read like a menu of all the past week's meals) unslung his heavy, double-barreled gun, stuck the muzzle right beneath my nose and asked, with a coarse laugh, how I liked his papalshooter. I had no idea what that was supposed to mean, but knew better than to admit it. The safest thing in such situations is to remain silent. And indeed, the next moment he confided in me that this high-powered repeater piece of his, equipped with a laser-finding telescopic sight, triple-action trigger and self-loader, was custom-made for killing popes. Talking continually, he pulled a folded photo from his pocket, a picture of himself taking careful aim at a mannequin in a robe and zucchetto. He had become an excellent shot, he said, and was now on his way to Rome, prepared for a great pilgrimage—to gun down the Holy Father at St. Peter's Basilica. I didn't believe a word of it, but then, still chattering away, he showed me, in turn, his airplane ticket, reservation, tourist missal, a pilgrim's itinerary for American Catholics, as well as a pack of cartridges with a cross carved on the head of each bullet. To economize he'd purchased a one-way ticket only, for he fully expected the enraged worshippers to tear him limb from limb—the prospect of which appeared to put him in the best possible humor. I immediately assumed that this was either a madman or a professional terrorist-fanatic (we have no lack of them these days), but again I was mistaken. Talking on and on, though he repeatedly had to climb off the high bar stool, for his weapon kept slipping to the floor, he revealed to me that actually he was a devout and loyal Catholic; the act which he had carefully planned—he called it "Operation P"—would be a great personal sacrifice, for he wished to jolt the conscience of the world, and what could provide a greater jolt than a deed of such extremity? He would be doing exactly what according to Scripture Abraham had been commanded to do to Isaac, except in reverse, as he would be slaying not a son, but a father, and a holy one at that. At the same time, he explained to me, he would attain the utmost martyrdom of which a Christian was capable, for his body would suffer terrible torment and his soul eternal damnation—all to open the eyes of mankind. "Really," I thought, "we have too many of these eye-opening enthusiasts." Unconvinced by his arguments, I excused myself and went to save the Pope—that is, to notify someone of this plot—but Stantor, whom I bumped into on the 77th floor bar, told me, without even hearing me out, that among the gifts offered to Hadrian XI by the last group of American tourists there had been two time bombs and a cask containing—not sacramental wine, but nitroglycerin. I understood Stantor's indifference a little better when I heard that the local guerrillas had recently mailed a foot to the

7

Embassy, though as yet it was uncertain whose. In the middle of our conversation they called him to the phone; it seemed that someone on the Avenida Romana had just set fire to himself in protest. The bar on the 77th had an entirely different atmosphere than the one up on mine: there were plenty of barefoot girls in waist-length fishnet dresses, some with sabres at their sides; a number of them had long braids fastened, in the latest fashion, to neck bands or spiked collars. I wasn't sure whether these were lady phillumenists or perhaps secretaries belonging to the Association of Liberated Publishers—though most likely it was the latter, judging from the color prints they were passing around. I went down nine floors to where our futurologists were staying, and in the bar there had a drink or two with Alphonse Mauvin of Agence France-Presse; for the last time I tried to save the Pope, but Mauvin received my story with stoicism, observing that only last month a certain Australian pilgrim had opened fire in the Vatican, albeit on entirely different ideological grounds. Mauvin was hoping for an interview with one Manuel Pyrhullo. This Pyrhullo was wanted by the FBI, Sûreté, Interpol, and a variety of other police organizations. It seems he had started a business which offered the public a new kind of service: that is, he hired himself out as a specialist-consultant on revolution through explosives (he was generally known under the pseudonym of "Dr. Boom"). Pyrhullo took great pride in the fact that his work was wholly nonpartisan. A pretty redhead wearing something that resembled a nightgown riddled with bullet holes approached our table; sent by the guerrillas, she was supposed to conduct a reporter to their headquarters. Mauvin, as he followed her out, handed me one of Pyrullo's fliers, from which I learned that it was high time to dispense with the bungling of irresponsible amateurs who couldn't tell dynamite from melinite, or fulminate mercury from a simple Bickford fuse. In these days of high specialization, the advertisement read, one attempted nothing on one's own, but placed one's trust in the expertise and integrity of certified professionals. On the back of the flier was a list of services, with prices given in the currencies of the world's most advanced and civilized nations.

Just then the futurologists began to congregate in the bar, but one of them, Professor Mashkenasus, ran in pale and trembling, claiming there was a time bomb in his room. The bartender, evidently accustomed to such episodes, automatically shouted "Hit the deck!" and dived under the counter. But the hotel detectives soon discovered that some colleague had played a practical joke on the Professor, placing an ordinary alarm clock in his cookie jar. It was probably an Englishman—only they delight in such childish pranks—but the whole thing was quickly forgotten when Stantor and J. G. Howler, also from UPI, came in with the text of a memo from the United States government to the government of Costa Rica with regard to the matter of the kidnapped diplomats. The language of it was typical of all such official communiqués; neither teeth nor feet were named. Jim told me that the local authorities might resort to drastic measures; General Apollon Diaz was currently in power and leaned toward the position of the hawks, which was to meet force with force. The proposal had already been made at Parliament (which stood in permanent emergency session) to counterattack: to pull twice the number of teeth from the political prisoners the abductors were demanding and mail them poste restante, as the address of guerrilla headquarters was unknown. The air edition of the *New York Times* ran an editorial (Schultzberger) calling for common sense and the solidarity of the human species. Stantor informed me in strictest confidence that the government had commandeered a train carrying secret military supplies—United States property—through Costa Rican territory on the way to Peru. Somehow the guerrillas hadn't yet hit upon the idea of kidnapping futurologists, which would certainly have made better sense from their point of view, inasmuch as there were many more futurologists than diplomats available in the country.

A hundred-story hotel is an organism so vast and so comfortably isolated from the rest of the world, that news from the outside filters in as if from another hemisphere. So far the futurologists hadn't panicked; the Hilton travel desk wasn't swamped by guests making flight reservations back to the States or elsewhere. The official banquet and opening ceremonies were scheduled for two, and still I hadn't changed into my evening pajamas, so I rushed up to my room, dressed and took an elevator down to the Purple Hall on the 46th. In the foyer two stunning girls in topless togas, their bosoms tattooed with forget-me-nots and snowflakes, came over and handed me a glossy folder. Without looking at it I entered the hall, which was still empty, and gasped at the sight of the tables—not because the spread was so extremely lavish, but the trays of hors d'oeuvres, the mounds of pâté, the molds, even the salad bowls, everything was arranged in the unmistakable shape of genitalia. For a moment I thought it might be my imagination, but a loudspeaker somewhere was playing a song, popular in certain circles, which began with the words: "Now to make it in the arts, publicize your private parts! Critics say you can't offend 'em with your phallus or pudendum!"

The first banqueters ambled in, gentlemen with thick beards and bushy whiskers, though they were really rather young, some in pajamas and some in nothing at all. When six waiters brought in the cake and I got a glimpse of that most indecent of desserts, there was no longer any doubt: I had accidentally strayed into the wrong hall and was sitting at the banquet for Liberated Literature. On the pretext that I couldn't find my secretary I beat a hasty retreat and took the elevator down a floor to the Purple Hall (I'd been in the Lavender), which by now was packed. My disappointment at the modesty of the reception I hid as best I could. It was a cold buffet, and there was nowhere to sit; all the chairs had been removed, so to eat anything one had to display an agility common to such occasions, particularly as there was an impossible crowd around the more substantial dishes. Señor Cuillone, a representative of the Costa Rican section of the Futurological Association, explained with an engaging smile that any sort of Lucullean abundance here would have been quite out of place, considering that a major topic of the conference was the imminent world famine facing humanity. Of course there were skeptics who said that the Association's allotments must have been cut, since only that could account for such heroic frugality. The journalists, long accustomed to doing without, busied themselves among us, seeking spot interviews with various foreign luminaries of prognostication. Instead of the United States ambassador, only the third secretary of the Embassy showed up, and with an enormous bodyguard; he was the only one wearing a tuxedo, perhaps because it would have been difficult to hide a bulletproof vest beneath a pair of pajamas. I learned that the guests from the city had been frisked in the lobby; supposedly there was already a growing pile of discovered weapons there. The meetings themselves were not to begin until five, which meant we had time to relax, so I returned to my room on the hundredth. I was terribly thirsty from the oversalted slaw, but since the bar on my floor had now been seized and occupied by the student protesters-dynamiters-and their girls—and anyway one conversation with that bearded papist (or antipapist) had been quite enough—I made do with a glass of water from the bathroom sink. The next thing I knew, all the lights were out, and the telephone, no matter what number I dialed, kept connecting me with an automated recording of the story of Rapunzel. I tried to take the elevator down, but it too was out of order. The students were singing in chorus, shooting their guns in time to the music—in the other direction, I hoped. Such things happen even in the best hotels, which doesn't make them any the less aggravating, yet what perplexed me the most were my own reactions. My mood, fairly sour since that conversation with the Pope's assassin, was now improving by the minute. Groping about in my room, I overturned some furniture and chuckled indulgently in the dark; even when I cracked my knee against a suitcase it didn't diminish my feeling of good will towards all mankind. On the night table I found the remains of the brunch I'd had sent up to my room, took one of the convention folders, rolled it up and stuck it in the leftover butter, then lit it with a match: that made a sort of torch—it sputtered and smoked, but gave enough light. After all, I had more than two hours to kill, counting on at least an hour on the staircase, since the elevator wasn't working. I sat back in an armchair and observed with the greatest interest the fluctuations and changes that were taking place within me. I was cheerful, I was never happier. No end of reasons for this wonderful state of affairs came rushing to my mind. In all seriousness it seemed to me that this hotel room, plunged in Stygian darkness, filled with stench and floating ashes from a homemade torch, totally cut off from the rest of the world, with a telephone that told fairy tales—was one of the nicest places on the face of the earth. Moreover I felt an irresistible urge to pat someone on the head, or at least squeeze a hand and look long and soulfully into a pair of eyes.

I would have embraced and kissed the most implacable enemy. The butter, melting, hissed and spat, and the thought that the *butter* might *sputter* and make the flame *gutter* was so hilarious that I burst out laughing, though my fingers were burnt relighting the paper whenever the torch went out. In the flickering light I hummed arias from old operettas, paying no heed to the bitter smoke that made me gag, or the tears streaming down my cheeks. Standing up, I tripped and fell, crashing into a trunk on the floor; the bump on my head swelled to the size of an egg, but that only put me in a better humor (to the extent that that was possible). I giggled, choking in the searing smoke, which in no way lowered my spirits. I climbed into bed; it still hadn't been made, though this was already the afternoon. The maids responsible for such neglect—I thought of them as my very own children: nothing but sugary words and gushing baby talk came to my lips. It occurred to me that even if I were to suffocate here, that would be the most amusing, the most agreeable kind of death any man could ask for. This thought was so blatantly contrary to my nature, that it had a sobering effect. A curious dissociation arose within me. As before, my soul was filled with light and languor, an all-embracing tenderness, a love of everything that existed, while my hands simply itched to fondle and stroke someone—it didn't matter who—till in the absence of any such third person I began to caress my own cheeks and chuck myself fondly under the chin; my right hand proffered itself to my left for a hearty shake. Even the feet, trembling eagerly, wanted to join in. And yet, throughout all this, distress signals were flashing on in the depths of my being: "Something's wrong!" cried a far-off, tiny voice inside. "Careful, Ijon, watch your step, be on your guard! This good weather can't be trusted! Come now, one-two-three, snap out of it! Don't sit there sprawled like some Onassis, weeping from the smoke, a bump on your head and universal lovingkindness in your heart! It's a trap, there's treachery afoot!" Though I didn't budge an inch. Yet my throat was exceedingly dry and the blood did pound in my ears (but that was due, no doubt, to the sudden rush of happiness). Driven by a powerful thirst, I got up to get another glass of water. I was thinking about the oversalted slaw at the banquet, and that dreadful buffet, then to experiment I thought about J. W., H. C. M. and M. W., my worst enemies—and discovered that beyond an impulse to clap them on the back, give them each a friendly hug, exchange a few kind words and kindred thoughts, I felt nothing whatever towards them. Now this was truly alarming. With one hand on the nickel spigot and the other holding the empty glass, I froze. Slowly I turned the water on, filled it, raised it, and then, twisting my face in a weird grimace—I could see the struggle in the bathroom mirror—I poured it down the drain.

*The water from the tap.* Of course. These changes in me had begun the moment I drank it. There was something in it, clearly. Poison? But I'd never heard of any poison that would . . . Wait a minute! I was, after all, a steady subscriber to all the major scientific publications. In just the last issue of *Science Today* there had been an article on some new psychotropic agents of the group of so-called *benignimizers* (the N,N-dimethylpeptocryptomides), which induced states of undirected joy and beatitude. Yes, yes! I could practically see that article now. Hedonidol, Euphoril, Inebrium, Felicitine, Empathan, Ecstasine, Halcyonal and a whole spate of derivatives! Though by replacing an amino group with a hydroxyl you obtained, instead, Furiol, Antagonil, Rabiditine, Sadistizine, Dementium, Flagellan, Juggernol, and many other polyparanoidal stimulants of the group of so-called phrensobarbs (for these prompted the most vicious behavior, the lashing out at objects animate as well as inanimate—and especially powerful here were the cannibal-cannabinols and manicomimetics).

My thoughts were interrupted by the telephone ringing, and then the lights came on again. A voice from some assistant manager at the reception desk humbly apologized for the inconvenience, with assurances that the malfunction had been located and corrected. I opened the door to air out the room—there wasn't a sound in the hall—and stood there, dizzy from the smoke and still filled with the desire to bless and caress. I shut the door, locked it, sat in the middle of the room and struggled to get a grip on myself. It is extremely difficult to describe my state at that time. The thoughts didn't come to me as easily or coherently as they may seem written here. Every analytical reflex was as if submerged in thick syrup, wrapped and smothered in a porridge of self-satisfaction, all dripping with the honey of idiotic optimism; my soul seemed to sink into the sweetest of oozes, like drowning in rosebuds and chocolate icing; I forced myself to think only of the most unpleasant things, the bearded maniac with the double-barreled papalshooter, the licentious publisher-procurers of Liberated Literature and their Babylonian hors d'oeuvres, and, of course, J. W., W. C. and J. C. M. and a hundred other villains and snakes in the grass—only to realize, with horror, that I loved them all, forgave them everything, and (what was worse) arguments kept popping into my head, arguments that defended every sort of evil and abomination. Bursting with love for my fellow man, I felt a driving need to lend a helping hand, to do good works. Instead of psychotropic poisons I greedily thought of the widows and orphans and with what pleasure I would watch over them forevermore. Ah, how shamefully had I neglected them in the past! And the poor, and the hungry, and the sick and destitute, Good Lord! I found myself kneeling over a suitcase, frantically pulling things out to find some article of value I could give to the needy. And once again the feeble voices of alarm called out desperately from my subconscious: "Attention! Danger! It's a trick, an ambush! Fight! Bite! Parry! Thrust! Help!" I was torn in two. I felt such a sudden surge of the categorical imperative, that I wouldn't have touched a fly. A pity, I thought, that the Hilton didn't have mice or even a few spiders. How I would have pampered the dear little things! Flies, fleas, rats, mosquitoes, bedbugs—all God's beloved, lovable creations! Meanwhile I blessed the table, the lamp, my own legs. But the vestiges of reason hadn't abandoned me altogether, so with my left hand I beat at the right, which was doing all the blessing, beat it until the pain made me writhe. Now that was encouraging! Perhaps there was hope after all! Luckily the desire to do good carried with it the wish for self-mortification. For a start, I punched myself in the mouth a couple of times; my ears rang and I saw stars. Good, excellent! When the face grew numb, I began kicking myself in the shins. Fortunately I had on heavy boots, with hard heels. After the therapeutic application of several swift kicks I felt much better—that is, much worse. Tentatively I tested the thought of how it would be to kick a certain C. A. as well. That no longer lay outside the realm of possibility. My shins ached like the blazes, and yet apparently it was thanks to the self-administered injury that I was now able to imagine the same dished out to old M. W. Ignoring the pain, I kicked on and on. Sharp objects were of use here too, and I availed myself of a fork and then some pins from an unused shirt. I was making progress, but there were setbacks; in a few minutes I was ready once again to immolate myself on the altar of some higher cause, all bubbling over with honor, virtue and noblesse oblige. Though I

**17**

knew full well that *something had been put in the water*. And then suddenly I remembered that there were sleeping pills in my suitcase—I carried them around with me but never used them, since they always left me feeling irritable and depressed. But now I took one, chewing it with a little soot-covered butter (water was out of the question, of course), then forced down two caffein pills—to counteract the sleeping pill —then sat and waited, full of dread but also full of boundless affection, waited for the outcome of this chemical war to be waged within my organism. Love seized me as never before, I was carried to unheard-of heights of generosity. Yet the chemicals of evil apparently were beginning to resist and push back the chemicals of goodness; I was still prepared to devote my life to charitable acts, but no longer without hesitation. Of course I would have felt more secure to have been a thorough scoundrel, if only for a while.

In about a quarter of an hour it was more or less over. I took a shower, rubbed myself vigorously with a towel, now and then—just to be on the safe side—slapped myself in the face, then applied bandaids to the cuts on my shins and fingers, inspected bruises (I had beaten myself black and blue in the course of this ordeal), put on a fresh shirt, a suit, adjusted my tie in the mirror, straightened my cape. Before leaving, I gave myself one good jab in the ribs—a final test—and then was out the door, right on time too, for it was almost five. To my great surprise everything seemed normal in the hotel. The bar on my floor was practically empty; the papalshooter was still there, propped up against a table, and I noticed two pair of feet, one pair bare, sticking out from under the counter, but that hardly suggested anything out of the ordinary. A couple of student militants were playing cards off to the side, and another was strumming his guitar and singing a popular song. The lobby downstairs literally swarmed with futurologists: they were all heading for the first session of the congress (without having to leave the Hilton, of course, since a hall had been reserved for that purpose in the lower part of the building). My surprise passed when I realized, upon reflection, that in such a hotel no one ever drank the water; if thirsty, they would have a coke, or a schweppes, and in a pinch there was always juice, tea or beer, or even soda water. All beverages came bottled. And even if someone should, out of carelessness, repeat my mistake, he wouldn't be out here, but up in his room behind locked doors, rolling on the floor in the throes of universal love. I concluded that it would be best for me to make no mention of this incident—I was new here, after all, and might not be believed. They would pass it off as a hallucination. And what could be more natural nowadays than to suspect someone of a fondness for drugs?

Afterwards I was criticized for following this oysterlike (or ostrichlike) policy, the argument being that, had I brought everything out in the open, the catastrophe might have been averted. Which is nonsense: at the very most I would have alerted the hotel guests, yet what took place at the Hilton had absolutely no effect on the march of political events in Costa Rica.

On the way to the convention hall I stopped at a newsstand and bought a batch of local papers, as is my habit. I don't buy them everywhere I go, of course, but an educated man can get the gist of something in Spanish, even if he doesn't speak the language.

Above the podium stood a decorated board showing the agenda for the day. The first item of business was the world urban crisis, the second—the ecology crisis, the third—the air pollution crisis, the fourth—the energy crisis, the fifth —the food crisis. Then adjournment. The technology, military and political crises were to be dealt with on the following day, after which the chair would entertain motions from the floor.

Each speaker was given four minutes to present his paper, as there were so many scheduled—198 from 64 different countries. To help expedite the proceedings, all reports had to be distributed and studied beforehand, while the lecturer would speak only in numerals, calling attention in this fashion to the salient paragraphs of his work. To better receive and process such wealth of information, we all turned on our portable recorders and pocket computers (which later would be plugged in for the general discussion). Stan Hazelton of the U.S. delegation immediately threw the hall into a flurry by emphatically repeating: 4, 6, 11, and therefore 22; 5, 9, hence 22; 3, 7, 2, 11, from which it followed that 22 and only 22!! Someone jumped up, saying yes but 5, and what about 6, 18, or 4 for that matter; Hazelton countered this objection with the crushing retort that, either way, 22. I turned to the number key in his paper and discovered that 22 meant the end of the world. Hayakawa from Japan was next; he presented plans, newly developed in his country, for the house of the future—eight hundred levels with maternity wards, nurseries, schools, shops, museums, zoos, theaters, skating rinks and crematoriums. The blueprints provided for underground storage of the ashes of the dear departed, forty-channel television, intoxication chambers as well as sobering tanks, special gymnasiums for group sex (an indication of the progressive attitude of the architects), and catacombs for nonconformist subculture communities. One rather novel idea was to have each family change its living quarters every day, moving from apartment to apartment like chessmen —say, pawns or knights. That would help alleviate boredom. In any event this building, having a volume of seventeen cubic kilometers, a foundation set in the ocean floor and a roof that reached the very stratosphere, would possess its own matrimonial computers—matchmaking on the sadomas-ochistic principle, for partners of such opposite persuasions statistically made the most stable marriages (each finding in that union the answer to his or her dreams)—and there would also be a round-the-clock suicide prevention center. Hakayawa, the second Japanese delegate, demonstrated for us a working model of such a house—on a scale of 10,000 to 1. It had its own oxygen supply, but without food or water reserves, since the building would operate entirely on the recycling principle: all waste products, excreta and effluvia, would be reclaimed and reprocessed for consumption. Yahakawa, the third on the team, read a list of all the del-icacies that could be reconstituted from human excrement. Among these were artificial bananas, gingerbread, shrimp, lobster, and even artificial wine which, notwithstanding its rather offensive origin, in taste rivaled the finest burgundies of France. Samples of it were available in the hall, in elegant little bottles, and there were also cocktail sausages wrapped in foil, though no one seemed to be particularly thirsty, and the sausages were discreetly deposited under chairs. Seeing which, I did the same. The original plan was to have this house of the future be mobile, by means of a powerful propeller, thereby making collective sightseeing excursions possible, but that was ruled out because, first of all, there would be 900 million houses to begin with and, secondly, all travel would be pointless. For even if a house had 1,000 exits and its occupants employed them all, they would never be able to leave the building; by the time the last was out, a whole new generation of occupants would have reached maturity inside.

The Japanese were clearly delighted with their own proposal. Then Norman Youhas from the United States took the floor and outlined seven different measures to halt the population explosion, namely: mass media and mass arrests, compulsory celibacy, full-scale deeroticization, onanization, sodomization, and for repeated offenders—castration. Every married couple would be required to compete for the right to have children, passing examinations in three categories, copulational, educational and nondeviational. All illegal offspring would be confiscated; for premeditated birth, the guilty parties could face life sentences. Attached to this report were those detachable sky-blue coupons—sex rations—we had received earlier with the conference materials. Hazelton and Youhas then proposed the establishment of new occupations: connubial prosecutor, divorce counselor, perversion recruiter and sterility consultant. Copies of a draft for a new penal code, in which fertilization constituted a major felony, tantamount to high treason against the species, were promptly passed around. Meanwhile someone in the spectator gallery hurled a Molotov cocktail into the hall. The police squad (on hand in the lobby, evidently prepared for such an eventuality) took the necessary steps, and a maintenance crew (no less prepared) quickly covered the broken furniture and corpses with a large nylon tarpaulin which was decorated in a cheerful pattern. Between reports I tried to decipher the local papers, and even though my Spanish was practically nonexistent, I did learn that the government had summoned armored units to the capital, put all law enforcement agencies on extreme alert, and declared a general state of emergency. Apparently no one in the audience besides myself grasped the seriousness of the situation developing outside the hotel walls. At seven we adjourned for supper—at our expense, this time—and on my way back to the conference I bought a special evening edition of *Nación*, the official newspaper, as well as a few of the opposition tabloids. Perusing these (with considerable difficulty), I was amazed to find articles full of saccharine platitudes on the theme of the tender bonds of love as the surest guarantee of universal peace—right beside articles that were full of dire threats, articles promising bloody repression or else an equally bloody insurrection. The only explanation I could think of for this peculiar incongruity was that some of the journalists had been drinking the water that day, and some hadn't. Of course less water would be consumed by the staff of a right-wing newspaper, since reactionary editors were better paid than their radical counterparts and consequently could afford to imbibe more exclusive liquids while they worked. The radicals, on the other hand, though they were known to display a certain degree of asceticism in the name of higher principles, hardly ever quenched their thirst with water. Especially since *quartzupio*, a fermented drink from the juice of the melmenole plant, was extremely cheap in Costa Rica.

We had settled back in our comfortable armchairs, and Professor Dringenbaum of Switzerland was just delivering the first numeral of his report, when all at once the hollow rumble of an explosion shook the building and made the windows rattle. The optimists among us passed this off as a simple earthquake, but I was inclined to think that the group of demonstrators outside that had been picketing the hotel since morning was now resorting to incendiary tactics. Though the following blast and concussion, much more powerful, changed my mind; now I could hear the familiar staccato of machine-gun fire in the streets. No, there was no longer any doubt: Costa Rica had entered into the stage of open hostilities. Our reporters were the first to disappear; at the sound of shooting they jumped to their feet and rushed out the door, eager to cover this new assignment. But Professor Dringenbaum went on with his lecture, which was fairly pessimistic in tone, for it maintained that the next phase of our civilization would be cannibalism. He cited several well-known American theoreticians, who had calculated that, if things on Earth continued at their present rate, in four hundred years humanity would represent a living sphere of bodies with a radius expanding at approximately the speed of light. But new explosions interrupted the report. The futurologists, confused, began to leave the hall and mingle in the lobby with people from the Liberated Literature convention. Judging by the appearance of these latter, the outbreak of the fighting had caught them in the middle of activity which suggested complete indifference to the threat of over-population. Behind some editors from the publishing house of Knopf stood naked secretaries—though not entirely naked, for their limbs were painted with various op designs. They carried portable water pipes and hookahs filled with a popular mixture of LSD, marijuana, yohimbine and opium. The liberationists, someone told me, had just burned the United States Postmaster General in effigy (it seems he had ordered the destruction of a pamphlet calling for the initiation of mass incest) and now, gathered in the lobby, they were be-having most inappropriately—particularly given the serious-ness of the situation. With the exception of a few who were exhausted or remained in a narcotic stupor, they all carried on in a positively scandalous fashion. I heard screams from the reception desk, where switchboard operators were being raped, and one potbellied gentleman in a leopardskin tore through the hotel cloakroom, waving a hashish torch as he chased the attendants. It took several porters to restrain him. Then someone from the mezzanine threw armfuls of photo-graphs down on our heads, photographs depicting in vivid color exactly how one man could satisfy his lust with another, and a great deal more besides. When the first tanks appeared in the streets—clearly visible from our windows —panic-stricken phillumenists and student protesters came pouring from the elevators; trampling underfoot the abovementioned pâté mounds and salad molds (which the publishers had brought out with them), these newcomers scattered in all directions. And there was the bearded anti-papist bellowing like a bull and wildly swinging his papalshooter, knocking down anyone who stood in the way. He pushed through the crowd and ran out in front of the hotel, where he hid behind a corner of the building and—I saw this with my own eyes—opened fire on the figures running past. Obviously this dedicated, ideologically motivated fanatic really didn't care, when it came down to it, whom he shot at. The lobby, filled with cries of terror and revelry, became a scene of utter pandemonium when the huge picture windows began to shatter. I tried to locate my reporter friends and, seeing them dash up the street, followed after; the atmosphere in the Hilton had really become too oppressive. Behind a low concrete wall along the hotel driveway crouched two cameramen, frantically filming everything, which made little sense, since everyone knows that the first thing that happens on such occasions is the burning of a car with foreign license plates. Flames and smoke were already rising from the hotel parking lot. Mauvin, standing beside me, rubbed his hands and chuckled at the sight of his Dodge crackling in the blaze—he had rented it from Hertz. The majority of the American reporters, however, did not find this amusing. I noticed some people struggling to put out the fire: these were mainly old men, poorly dressed, and they were hauling water in buckets from a nearby fountain. That struck me as odd. In the distance, at the far end of the Avenida del Salvación and the Avenida del Resurrección, police helmets glimmered; yet the square in front of the hotel, with its surrounding lawns and luxuriant palms, was still empty. Those doddering old men, hoarsely calling to one another, quickly formed a fire brigade, in spite of their canes and crutches; such gallantry was astounding, but then I remembered what had happened earlier that day and immediately shared my suspicions with Mauvin. The rattle of machine guns and the thunder of bursting shells made it difficult to talk; for a while the Frenchman's keen face showed a total lack of comprehension, but suddenly his eyes lit up. "Aha!" he roared above the din. "The water! The drinking water! Great God, for the first time in history . . . *cryptochemocracy!*" And with these words he ran back to the hotel like one possessed. To get to a telephone, apparently. Strange though, that the lines should still be open.

I was standing there in the driveway when Professor Trottelreiner, one of the Swiss futurologists, joined me. By then the police were doing what they should have done hours ago: wearing black helmets, shields and gas masks, armed with guns and clubs, they formed a cordon around the whole Hilton complex to keep back the mob, which was just beginning to pour from the park that separated us from the city's theater district. With great skill special police units set up grenade launchers and fired these into the crowd; the explosions were remarkably weak, though they raised thick clouds of whitish smoke. At first I thought that this was tear gas, but the people, instead of fleeing and choking in fury, clearly began to huddle around the pale vapors; their shouts quickly died away, and soon I could hear them singing—they were singing hymns. The reporters, rushing back and forth between the cordon and the hotel entrance with their cameras and tape recorders, were completely mystified by this, though it was obvious to me that the police were employing some new pacification chemical, in aerosol form. But then, from the Avenida del . . . I can't recall which . . . another group of people appeared, and these were somehow unaffected by the grenades, or so it seemed. Later I was told that this group had continued advancing in order to help the police, not to attack them. Yet who could draw such subtle distinctions in that general chaos? There were several more salvos of grenades, and that was followed by the characteristic roar and hiss of a water cannon, then finally the machine guns opened up and the air was filled with the whine of bullets. They were playing for keeps now, so I ducked behind the low driveway wall, using it like the breastwork of a trench, and found myself between Stantor and Haynes of the *Washington Post*. In a few words I filled them in; they were furious that I had betrayed such a banner-headline secret first to an AFP man, and crawled full speed back to the hotel, only to return shortly, scowling—the lines were no longer open. But Stantor had managed to buttonhole the officer in charge of hotel defenses and learned from him that planes carrying LTN bombs (LTN: Love Thy Neighbor) were now on their way. Then we were ordered to clear the area, and all the policemen put on gas masks with special filters. We received masks too.

Professor Trottelreiner was, as luck would have it, a specialist in the field of psychotropic pharmacology, and he cautioned me not to use the gas mask under any circumstance, as it would cease to operate at sufficiently high concentrations of aerosol; this would then give rise to the so-called phenomenon of filter overload, and in an instant one could inhale a much heavier dose than if one breathed the air without the benefit of a mask. The only sure protection, he said, anticipating my question, would be a separate oxygen supply; so we went to the hotel desk, managed to catch one receptionist still on duty and found, with his assistance, a storeroom full of fire-fighting equipment, including plenty of oxygen masks: Draeger make, with closed circulation. Thus accoutered, the Professor and I returned to the street, just in time to hear the dreadful, ear-splitting whistle that announced the arrival of the first planes. As everyone knows, the Hilton was accidentally bombed with LTN minutes after the air raid commenced; the consequences of that error were disastrous. True, the LTN hit only the far wing of the building's lower structure, where display booths had been set up by the Association of Publishers of Liberated Literature, and therefore none of the hotel guests suffered immediate injury. On the other hand, the police guarding us took the full brunt of it. Paroxysms of love soon swept their ranks, assuming mass proportions. Before my eyes policemen tore the masks from their faces and, shedding copious tears of remorse, fell to their knees and begged the demonstrators for forgiveness, pushing the billy clubs into their hands with fervent pleas to be severely beaten. Following another LTN bombardment, which raised the drug's concentration even more, these minions of the law stumbled over themselves in the mad rush to kiss and hug everyone within reach. It was only several weeks after the whole tragedy that we were able, more or less, to piece together what had happened. The government had decided that morning to nip the developing revolution in the bud, so it put into the municipal water tower about 700 kilograms of bromo-benignimizer, mixing equal parts of Felicitine, Placidol and Superjubilan. The water to the police and military barracks had been shut off first, of course. Except that without the proper experts this plan was doomed to failure—the phenomenon of filter overload in the masks was not taken into account, for example, nor the fact that different social groups would consume the drinking water in radically different amounts.

The conversion of the police took place with particular violence because, as Trottelreiner explained to me, the less an individual was accustomed to following his own natural good impulses, the greater the effect of such drugs upon him. That explained why, when two planes in the next wave accidentally LTN'd the city hall, so many of the highest ranking police and military officials committed suicide, unable to endure the terrible pangs of conscience over policies they had implemented in the past. And if you add to this the fact that General Diaz himself had—before putting a bullet through his head—ordered the immediate release of all political prisoners, it is easier to understand the extraordinary ferocity of the fighting that developed in the course of the night. The airstrips, being far from the city, remained untouched, and the pilots had their orders, and followed them to the letter. Police and military observers in their hermetic bunkers, seeing what was going on, finally resorted to the extreme measures that plunged all Nounas into the chaos of total emotional derangement. Of course we had no inkling of any of this at the Hilton. It was eleven o'clock at night when the first armored divisions of the army appeared on the scene, rolling into the square surrounded by parks and palms; they had come to stifle the brotherly love rampant among the police. This they did, with considerable bloodshed. Poor Mauvin was standing a foot away from the place where a pacification grenade exploded; the force of the blast tore the fingers off his left hand as well as his left ear, but he assured me that he had never really cared for that hand in the first place and the ear wasn't worth mentioning, in fact if I liked I could have the other, and he pulled a penknife from his pocket to make good the offer; but I took the penknife gently from his hand and led him to an improvised first-aid station. There he was tended by the secretaries of the liberated publishers; now chemically converted, they were all bawling like babies. They had put on modest clothing and even wore veils, so as not to tempt anyone to sin; a few of these pitiful creatures, more strongly affected, had actually shaven their heads. On the way back from the first-aid area I had the miserable luck to run into a group of publishers. Though I didn't recognize them at first: they were dressed in old burlap bags tied around with rope (which they also used to flog themselves); crying for mercy, clamoring, they threw themselves at my feet and beseeched me to whip them properly, for they had depraved society. Imagine my surprise when, looking at these flagellants more closely, I saw that they were all from the staff of *Playboy*, including the editor in chief! That gentleman wouldn't let me go, so bitterly did his conscience torment him. They pulled at my sleeves, realizing that thanks to the oxygen mask I was the only one able to harm a hair on their head. I could take no more of this and gave in to their demands at last, much against my will. Soon my arms were aching, and it grew difficult to breathe—I was afraid I might not find another tank of oxygen when this one ran out—meanwhile the publishers had formed a long line, trembling with impatience for their turn. Finally, to get rid of them, I told them to pick up all those enormous color posters that had been thrown into the lobby by the LTN explosions in the wing of the Hilton, that made the place look like Sodom and Gomorrah twice over; following my instructions, they put the posters in a huge pile out in front of the hotel and burned them. Unfortunately an artillery unit stationed in the park took the bonfire for some kind of signal and opened up on us. I left as quickly as I could, only to bump into one Harvey Simsworth in the basement. This was a writer who had hit upon the lucrative idea of turning fairy tales into hardcore pornography (he was the author of *Ali Baba and the Forty Perverts*), then made another fortune by rewriting the classics of world literature (works like *King Leer*); he employed the simple device of revealing the "secret sex life" of all the traditional tales—for example, what Snow White really did with the seven dwarfs, what Jack did with Jill, what Aladdin did with his lamp, etc., etc. I tried to beg off, explaining that my arm was tired. In that case—he shouted, sobbing—I could at least kick him. What could I do? It was heartless to refuse. Later, completely worn out by these exertions, I dragged myself back to the room with the fire extinguishers, where luckily I found a couple more un-used cylinders of oxygen. Professor Trottelreiner was there, seated on a coil of fire hose; he was reading the futurological articles, glad to have found a little free time in the professional hustle and bustle of attending conferences. Meanwhile the LTN bombs continued to fall thick and fast. The Professor advised that in severe cases of lovestroke—and especially serious was an attack of universal good will, accompanied by petting convulsions—poultices should be applied, as well as heavy doses of castor oil in alternation with the pumping of the stomach.

In the newsroom Stantor, Wooley (from the *Herald*), Sharkey and Kuntze (a photographer working temporarily for *Paris-Match*) were playing cards with masks on their faces. Since the lines were out, they had nothing better to do. I began to watch, but Joe Missinger, an important American journalist, burst in yelling that the police had been given tablets of Furiol to counteract the benignimizers. We understood at once what that meant and ran for the basement, but it turned out to be another false rumor. So we went outside to look around; I made the dismal discovery that our hotel was missing its top twenty or thirty floors; my room, along with everything in it, was lost in a mountain of rubble. Flames filled three quarters of the sky. A burly policeman in a helmet was chasing some youth, roaring: "Stop, stop for God's sake, *I love you!*"—but the youth ignored these exhortations. Things had quieted down somewhat, and the reporters, driven by their professional urge to investigate, cautiously headed for the park. I went along. There were a variety of religious services in progress, black masses and white, with the secret police participating conspicuously. Nearby stood a large crowd of people weeping and tearing their hair; they were holding over their heads an enormous sign which read, SPIT ON US, WE ARE INFORMERS! Judging by the number of these penitent Judases, it must have cost the government plenty to maintain them—funds which might have been better spent improving the economic situation in Costa Rica. Back at the Hilton we saw another crowd. Police dogs, behaving more like friendly Saint Bernards, were trotting out bottles of the most expensive liquor from the hotel bar and distributing them indiscriminately. In the bar itself policemen and protesters, arms around one another, took turns singing patriotic and revolutionary songs. I tried the basement, but couldn't endure all the converting and cavorting going on in there, so I went to the room with the fire extinguishers to talk to Professor Trottelreiner. To my surprise, he had found three partners and was playing bridge. Quetzalcoatl, a graduate student, trumped his ace; this so angered the Professor that he left the table in a huff. Just then Sharkey stuck his head in the door and announced that he had caught General Aquillo's speech on the radio: they were going to crush the rebellion by dropping conventional bombs on the city. After a brief council of war we decided to retreat to the lowest level of the Hilton, which was an underground sewer system. The hotel kitchen having been totally demolished, there was nothing to eat; hungry demonstrators, phillumenists and publishers stuffed themselves with the chocolate lozenges, aspics and other morsels they had discovered in the abandoned *centro erotico* at the corner of the hotel wing. I saw how their faces changed when the sexual stimulants contained in those comestibles began to mix in their veins with the benignimizers. One shuddered to think where this chemical escalation might lead. I saw the pairing off of futurologists with Indian bootblacks, I saw secret agents in the arms of hotel janitors, and enormous sleek rats fraternizing with cats—while the police dogs licked everyone and everything in sight. Our progress was slow and difficult, for we had to push our way through a heavy crowd, and I was bringing up the rear, struggling with half the oxygen tanks on my back. Patted, kissed on the arms and legs, fondled and adored, smothered by hugs and squeezes, I stubbornly plowed ahead, until I heard Stantor shout in triumph: he'd found the entrance to the sewers! Exerting the last of our strength, we moved aside the heavy manhole cover and lowered ourselves one by one into the concrete well. I held Professor Trottelreiner, whose foot had slipped on a rung of the iron ladder, and asked him if he'd ever imagined the convention turning out like this. Instead of answering, he tried to kiss my hand, which immediately aroused my suspicions; his mask had been knocked loose, as it turned out, causing him to swallow some of the drug-contaminated air. Without delay we applied physical torture, forced him to breathe pure oxygen, and read Hayakawa's report aloud —that was Howler's idea. The Professor finally came to his senses, of which he gave ample evidence by a series of pungent oaths, and we were able to continue on our way. Suddenly in the dim beam of our flashlight we saw the dark wall of the sewer covered with patches of oil; this was a most welcome sight, for now thirty feet of earth separated us from the surface of the LTN'd city. Imagine our surprise when we discovered that we had not been the first to think of this haven. There on the concrete platform sat, in full assembly, the management of the Hilton; these prudent officials had provided themselves with inflatable reclining chairs from the hotel pool, transistor radios, plenty of scotch and bourbon, and an ample picnic lunch. Since they too were wearing oxygen masks, there was little chance, if any, that they would willingly share their provisions with us. But we assumed a threatening attitude and managed to convince them (they were outnumbered anyway). And so with a little arm-twisting full agreement was reached, and we all sat down to dine on cold lobster. This meal, unscheduled and unforeseen in the program, concluded the first day of the futurological congress.

*

Quite exhausted by the stormy events of the day, we settled down for the night in more than Spartan circumstances, considering that we were obliged to sleep on a narrow concrete platform that bore the unmistakable traces of the sewer. The first problem that arose was to divide up fairly the reclining chairs, which the hotel directors had so thoughtfully brought with them. There were six chairs, accomodating twelve persons, for the six-membered management team had planned to share this bedding (in the spirit of camaraderie) with its private secretaries; while those of us who had entered the sewer under Stantor's leadership numbered twenty. That included the futurological group of Professors Dringenbaum, Hazelton and Trottelreiner, several reporters and television commentators from CBS, and two individuals enlisted along the way, a muscular man in a leather jacket and riding boots (no one knew who he was) and little Josephine Collins, girl Friday to the editor of *Playboy*. Stantor evidently intended to profit from her chemical conversion; he had already gotten her to agree, so I heard, to sign over the first rights to her memoirs. With six chairs and thirty-odd applicants, the situation became explosive. We lined up on either side of these makeshift beds and glowered at one another, to the extent that one can glower in an oxygen mask. Somebody proposed that on the count of three we all remove our masks; in that way, obviously, everyone would be overcome with altruism, and there would then be no contention. However, no one seemed particularly anxious to put this plan into action. After a great deal of bickering we finally reached a compromise: we would draw lots and sleep in three-hour shifts. For lots we used those booklets of sky-blue copulation coupons some of us still carried on our person. It turned out that I got the first shift, along with Professor Trottelreiner, who was a bit more gaunt and angular than I would have liked, since we had to sleep together in the same bed, or rather chair. The ones who were next woke us roughly, and while they made themselves comfortable in our place we squatted at the edge of the sewer and nervously checked the pressure in our cylinders. The oxygen wouldn't last more than a few hours, that much was clear. The grim prospect of becoming benignimized seemed inevitable. Gloom descended upon us. Knowing that I had already had a taste of that state of bliss, my companions anxiously inquired how it felt. I assured them that it wasn't so bad really, but I spoke without conviction. Sleep overpowered us; to keep from falling into the sewer we tied ourselves, with whatever we could, to the iron rungs beneath the manhole. Dozing fitfully, I was awakened by the sound of an explosion far more powerful than anything yet; I looked around in the darkness—all the flashlights but one had been turned off, to conserve the batteries. Enormous sleek rats trotted by along the edge of the sewer. The odd thing was that they were walking single file, and on their hind legs. I pinched myself, but no, it wasn't a dream. I woke Professor

Trottelreiner and showed him this phenomenon; he didn't know what to make of it. The rats were now walking in pairs, completely ignoring our presence; at least they weren't attempting to lick us, which the Professor considered a good sign, since it indicated that in all probability the air was clean. Cautiously we removed our masks. Both journalists on my right were sleeping soundly while the rats continued to promenade on two legs, but then the Professor and I sneezed, something was tickling our nostrils—the sewer stench, I thought at first, until I noticed the roots. I bent over to look at my feet. There was no mistake, I was sending out roots all right—from the knees down, more or less—and turning green above. And now my arms were sprouting buds, which opened quickly, unfolding before my very eyes. It's true the leaves were rather pale, but that is usually the case with plants grown underground. I had the feeling that any minute I should start bearing fruit. I wanted to ask Trottelreiner what he thought of this, but had to raise my voice, he was rustling so much. The sleepers meanwhile resembled a clipped hedge strewn with lilac and scarlet flowers. The rats nibbled at the foliage, smoothed their whiskers with their paws, and grew even larger. A little more, I thought, and one might ride them. Like a tree I yearned for the sun. As if from a great distance intermittent thunder reached my ears, something was falling gently, there was a rumbling, like echoes in corridors, and I turned red, then gold, then finally my leaves flew away in the wind. What—I wondered, surprised—was it autumn already?

If so, then it was time to be off; I pulled up roots and cocked an ear. Ah yes, there were the trumpets sounding. A rat with a saddle—a truly remarkable specimen, for a rodent—turned its head and, blinking its heavy, slanting lids, looked at me with the mournful eyes of Professor Trottelreiner. I hesitated, struck by a sudden doubt; if this was the Professor with the features of a rat, it would hardly be proper to mount him; on the other hand if this was merely a rat that bore some resemblance to the Professor, there was nothing to worry about. But the trumpets were sounding again, so I leaped into the saddle—and fell in the sewer. The foul water restored me to my senses at last. Shuddering with disgust and indignation, I crawled back onto the platform. The rats reluctantly made room for me. They were still walking about on two legs. But of course—it dawned on me—hallucinogens! If I could think I was a tree, why couldn't they think they were people? Hurriedly I groped around for my oxygen mask, found it, put it on, breathing in however with some misgiving, for how could I be sure that it was a real mask, and not an illusion?

Suddenly there was light all around me; I raised my head and saw that the manhole was open; an American sergeant was holding out his hand.

"Come on!" he yelled. "Come on!"

"What, have the helicopters arrived?!" I jumped to my feet.

"Quickly!" he yelled. "There's not a second to lose!"

The others were up now too. I climbed the ladder.

"It's about time!" Stantor wheezed beneath me.

Outside the sky was bright with fire. I looked—no helicopters, only a few soldiers in helmets and dressed like paratroopers. They handed us some kind of harness.

"What is it?" I asked, confused.

"Quickly, quickly!" yelled the sergeant.

The soldiers began to saddle me with the thing. "I'm hallucinating!" I thought.

"Not at all," said the sergeant. "These are jump holsters, our individual rocket carriers, the fuel tank's in the backpack. Here, grab this." And he shoved some kind of lever into my hand, while a soldier standing behind me tightened the shoulder straps and belt. "There!"

The sergeant clapped me on the back and pushed a button. There was a long, piercing whistle and white smoke poured from the pack's nozzle, enveloping my legs. In an instant I was borne into the air like a feather.

"But I don't know how to steer it!" I shouted as I soared up into the flickering, blazing night.

"You'll learn!" called the sergeant from below. "Take your azimuth—from—the—Nooorth—Staaar!!"

I looked down. I was flying over the gigantic pile of rubble which not too long ago had been the Hilton. Near it was a tiny cluster of people, and farther on a bursting blood-red ring of fire that silhouetted some object, small and round—it was Professor Trottelreiner blasting off, his umbrella open. I checked to see if my straps and buckles were holding properly. The power pack gurgled, clanged, hissed, the propelling column of steam began to burn my calves, so I drew up my knees as far as possible, but this made me lose stability and for a full minute I was spinning in the air like a lopsided top. But then without thinking I clutched at the lever, which must have changed the direction of the jets, because the next thing I knew I was horizontal and cruising comfortably, even pleasantly—though it would have been a lot more enjoyable had I had the least idea of where I was going. I maneuvered the lever, trying at the same time to take in the whole scene that lay below. Ruins of buildings, like dark fangs, stood outlined against rising walls of flame. Thin filaments of fire—blue, red, green—came rushing up from the ground to meet me, went screaming by, and I realized that I was being shot at. Quickly as I could, I pushed the lever. The power pack coughed and whined like a broken boiler, it scalded my legs and hurled me head over heels into pitch-black space. The wind whistled in my ears, I felt the wallet, penknife and other odds and ends slip out of my pockets, and tried to dive after them, but they had vanished from sight. Alone beneath the silent stars, still hissing, sputtering, clanging, I flew on. I looked for the North Star, to get my bearings, but by the time I'd found it the power pack gave a last gasp and down I went like a stone, picking up speed. By the greatest stroke of luck, just above the ground—I could see a pale, winding highway, shadows of trees, some rooftops—an unexpected spurt from the nozzle broke my fall enough to let me land, and quite softly too, on the grass. Someone lay in a ditch nearby and groaned. It would be strange indeed, I thought, if that was the Professor! And yet it really was he. I helped him up. He felt himself all over, complaining that he'd lost his glasses. Though otherwise he seemed all right. He asked me to assist him in removing his pack. He crouched over it and pulled out something from a side pocket—steel tubes and a wheel.

"And now yours . . ."

From my pack too he took a wheel, fiddled awhile and finally cried:

"Hop on! Let's go!"

"What is it? Where are we going?" I asked, amazed.

"A tandem bicycle. To Washington," the Professor laconically replied, his foot already on the pedal.

"I'm hallucinating!" flashed through my mind.

"Nonsense!" huffed Trottelreiner. "It's standard paratroop equipment."

"All right, but how are you such an expert on this?" I asked, climbing onto the back seat. The Professor kicked off and we drove along the grass to where the asphalt began.

"I work for the USAF!" he said, pedaling like mad.

Now as far as I could recall, Peru and Mexico lay between us and Washington, not to mention Panama.

"We'll never make it by bicycle!" I shouted against the wind.

"Only to the rendezvous point!" the Professor shouted back.

Was he then not the simple futurologist he seemed? Oh, what had I gotten myself into this time? Something big, no doubt . . . And anyway, what business did I have in Washington? I started to brake.

"What are you doing?" growled the Professor, hunched over the handlebars. "Keep going!"

"No, I'm getting off!" I said, my mind made up.

The bicycle slowed and came to a stop. The Professor, putting a foot on the ground to support himself, showed me the surrounding darkness with a sarcastic sweep of the hand.

"As you wish. Good hunting!"

And he was on his way again.

"Thanks for everything!" I called out after him as the red

glow of his taillight vanished in the night. Thoroughly disoriented, I sat on a milepost to gather my thoughts.

Something was jabbing me in the calf. Absent-mindedly I reached down and, feeling some branches, began to break them off. It hurt. "If those are *my* branches," I told myself, "then this is definitely still a hallucination!" I was bending over to see, when a bright beam hit me in the face. Silver headlights came swerving around the corner, the enormous shadow of a car pulled up, and a door swung open. Inside —blue, green, golden rows of lights flashing on a dashboard, a pair of shapely legs in nylons, alligator slippers resting on the accelerator, a dark face with crimson lips turned in my direction, and sparkling diamonds on the fingers that held the steering wheel.

"Need a lift?"

I got in. I was so stunned that I had forgotten about the branches. Secretly I ran a hand along my legs. They were only twigs.

"What, already?" she asked in a low, sensuous voice.

"What do you mean?" I said, completely at a loss.

She shrugged. The powerful car surged forward, the lighted strip of road rushed towards us out of the darkness; she pushed a button and a lively tune flowed from under the dashboard. And yet, I thought, it didn't fit somehow. It didn't make sense. True, they weren't branches, only twigs. But even so!

I looked her over. She was beautiful all right, beautiful in a way that was at once seductive, demonic, and raspberry. But instead of a skirt she had feathers. Ostrich? Was I hallucinating? . . . Women's fashions being what they were, I didn't know what to think. The road was deserted; we tore along until the needle on the speedometer leaned all the way to the right. Suddenly a hand from behind clutched my hair. I jumped. But the long nails were clawing the back of my neck affectionately rather than with murderous intent.

"Who's that?" I tried to pull free, but couldn't. "Let go of me, please!"

Lights flickered up ahead, a big house loomed, gravel crunched beneath our tires, then the car made a sharp turn, drew up to a curb and stopped.

The hand that still held me by the hair belonged to another woman; she was pale, slender, dressed in black and wearing sunglasses. The car door flew open.

"Where are we?" I asked.

Without a word they pounced and, with the one at the wheel pushing and the other—already on the sidewalk —pulling, I was forced from the car. There was a party going on in the house, I heard music, drunken shouts, and the fountain near the driveway ran yellow and purple in the light of the windows. My companions took me firmly by the arms.

"But I really don't have the time," I muttered.

They paid no attention. The one in black leaned over and whispered, her hot breath in my ear:

'Hoo!"

"I beg your pardon?"

By now we were at the door; they both began to laugh, apparently at me. Everything about them was repulsive, and besides that, they were growing smaller. Kneeling? No, their legs were covered with feathers. "Aha!" I said to myself, not without relief. "Then it *is* a hallucination after all!"

"Hallucination, is it?" snorted the one in the sunglasses. She raised her handbag beaded with black pearls and hit me over the head. I groaned.

"I'll give you a hallucination, dungbutt!" screamed the other, and dealt me a savage blow in the very same place. I fell, covering my head with my arms. I opened my eyes. Professor Trottelreiner was bending over me, his umbrella in his hand. I was lying on the sewer platform. The rats were walking in pairs as if nothing had happened.

"Where, where does it hurt you?" inquired the Professor. "Here?"

"No, here . . ." I showed him the lump on my head.

He lifted the point of his umbrella and jabbed me in the injured place.

"Help!" I yelled. "Please, no more! Why are you—"

"Helping you is precisely what I'm trying to do!" said the futurologist sternly. "Unfortunately, I have no other antidote at hand!"

"At least not with the point, for God's sake!"

"It's more efficacious that way."

He struck once more, turned and called someone. I closed my eyes. My head throbbed. Then I felt a tugging. The Professor and the man in the leather jacket took hold of my arms and legs and began to carry me somewhere.

"Where now?" I cried.

Bits of rubble dribbled down on my face from the trembling ceiling; I felt my bearers stepping along some shaky board or plank and shuddered, afraid they might slip. "Where are you taking me?" I asked feebly, but there was no answer. The air was filled with incessant thunder. Then it grew bright, and we were outside, fire all around; men in uniform were seizing everyone brought out of the sewer and pushing them rather roughly, one by one, through an open door—I got a glimpse of the large white letters U.S. ARMY COPTER 1-109-894—then I was lying on a stretcher. Professor Trottelreiner stuck his head inside the helicopter window.

"Sorry, Tichy old boy!" he shouted. "It was necessary!"

Someone standing behind him tore the umbrella from his hand, whacked the Professor twice over the head, and shoved him in among us; the futurologist fell to the floor with a groan. Meanwhile the rotors whirred, the motors roared, and the machine lifted majestically into the air. The Professor took a seat by my stretcher, gingerly rubbing the back of his head. I confess that though I fully understood the charitableness of his actions, it was with some satisfaction that I noticed the bump swelling there.

"Where are we going?"

"To the futurological congress," said Trottelreiner, still wincing.

"But . . . wasn't it—isn't it over?"

"Washington stepped in," he explained laconically. "We're continuing the conference."

"Where?"

"Berkeley."

"You mean, the university?"

"Right. You wouldn't happen to have a penknife on you?"

"No."

The helicopter lurched, burst into flames. An explosion ripped open the cabin and we were flung out into the void. There was a great deal of pain after that. I seemed to hear the long wail of a siren, someone was cutting my clothes with scissors, I blacked out, I regained consciousness again. Shaken by a fever and a bumpy road, I was looking at the dull white ceiling of an ambulance. Next to me lay another body, bandaged like a mummy; by the umbrella tied to it I recognized Professor Trottelreiner. It occurred to me that I was still alive. So by some miracle we had survived that terrible fall. Suddenly the ambulance swerved and skidded, tires screeching—turned over, burst into flames, and an explosion ripped apart its metal frame. "What, again?" was my final thought before I sank into oblivion. When I opened my eyes, I saw a glass dome over me; some people in white, wearing masks, their arms raised like priests giving benedictions, were conferring in lowered tones.

"Yes, this was Tichy," came the words. "We'll put it here, in the jar. No, no, only the brain. The rest is useless. Now the anesthetic, please."

A nickel ring lined with cotton shut out everything; I wanted to scream, to call for help, but inhaled the stinging gas and floated off into nothingness. When I woke again, I was unable to open my eyes, unable to move my arms or legs, as if I had been paralyzed. I redoubled my efforts in spite of the pain.

"Easy there! Don't struggle!" said a soothing, melodious voice.

"What? Where am I? What's wrong with me?" I blurted out. My lips felt odd, my whole face.

"You're in a hospital. Everything's fine. There's absolutely nothing to worry about. In just a minute we'll give you something to eat . . ."

"But how can I, if I don't have any . . ." I was about to say, but heard the snipping of scissors. Whole swaths of gauze fell from my face; it grew brighter. Two hulking orderlies took me gently but firmly under the arms and set me on my feet. I was astonished at their size. They helped me into a wheelchair. Before me steamed an appetizing broth. Reaching automatically for the spoon, I noticed that the hand that picked it up was small and black as ebony. I inspected this hand. Seeing that it moved exactly as I wished, I was forced to conclude that it was my own. And yet it had changed so much. I looked around to ask someone the reason and my eyes fell on a mirror on the opposite wall. There in a wheelchair sat an attractive young black woman, bandaged up, in pajamas, an expression of dismay on her face. I touched my nose. The reflection in the mirror did the same. I felt my face all over, my neck, but when I came to the bosom I cried out in alarm. My voice was high and reedy.

"Good Lord!"

The nurse scolded someone for not covering up the mirror, then turned to me and said:

"You are Ijon Tichy?"

"Yes. That is—yes, yes!! But what does this mean? That lady—that black woman—"

"A transplant. There was no other way. We had to save your life, and saving your life meant—well, your brain!" The nurse spoke quickly but clearly, holding both my hands in hers. I closed my eyes. I opened them, suddenly feeling very weak. The surgeon burst in with a look of the greatest indignation.

"What's going on here?" he roared. "The patient could fall into shock!"

"He already has!" returned the nurse. "It was Simmons, Doctor. I told him to cover the mirror!"

"Shock? Then what are you waiting for? Take him to surgery!" ordered the doctor.

"No! I've had enough!" I yelled.

But no one listened to my woman's pleas and squeals. A white sheet fell across my face. I tried to tear free, but couldn't. I heard and felt the rubber wheels of the hospital cart rolling along a tiled floor. Then there was a terrible blast, the sound of windows shattering, flames and smoke. An explosion rocked the corridor.

"It's a demonstration! Protesters!" someone cried. Broken glass crunched beneath the shoes of people fleeing. Helplessly trapped in the sheet, I felt a sharp pain in my side and lost consciousness.

I came to and found myself in jam. Cranberry jam, awfully sour. I was lying on my stomach, with something large and fairly soft crushing me. A mattress. I kicked it off. Pieces of brick were digging into my knees and palms. I propped myself up, spitting out cranberry pits and sand. The room looked as though a bomb had hit it. The window frames jutted out, jagged slivers of glass protruding from their edges, pointing to the floor. The overturned hospital bed was charred. Near me lay a large printed card, smeared with jam. I picked it up and read:

*Dear Patient (first name, last name)! You are presently located in our experimental state hospital. The measures taken to save your life were drastic, extremely drastic (circle one). Our finest surgeons, availing themselves of the very latest achievements of modern medicine, performed one, two, three, four, five, six, seven, eight, nine, ten operations (circle one) on you. They were forced, acting wholly in your interest, to replace certain parts of your organism with parts obtained from other persons, in strict accordance with Federal Law (Rev. Stat. Comm. 1-989/0-001/89/1). The notice you are now reading was thoughtfully prepared in order to help you make the best possible adjustment to these new if somewhat unexpected circumstances in your life, which, we hasten to remind you, we have saved. Although it was found necessary to remove your arms, legs, spine, skull, lungs, stomach, kidneys, liver, other (circle one or more), rest assured that these mortal remains were disposed of in a manner fully in keeping with the dictates of your religion; they were, with the proper ritual, interred, embalmed, mummified, buried at sea, cremated with the ashes scattered in the wind—preserved in an urn—thrown in the garbage (circle one). The new form in which you will henceforth lead a happy and healthy existence may possibly occasion you some surprise, but we promise that in time you will become, as indeed all our dear patients do, quite accustomed to it. We have supplemented your organism with the very best, the best, perfectly functional, adequate, the only available (circle one) organs at our disposal, and they are fully guaranteed to last a year, six months, three months, three weeks, six days (circle one). Of course you must realize that . . .*

Here the text broke off. It was only then that I saw my

name written in block letters across the top of the card: IJON TICHY, Operations 6, 7 and 8, COMBO. The paper shook in my hands. Good Lord, I thought, what was left of me? I was afraid to look, even at my own finger. There was thick red hair on the back of the hand. Dizzy and trembling all over, I got up, holding on to the wall for support. No bosom—well at least that was something. Complete silence, except for a bird chirping outside. A fine time to chirp! COMBO. What did COMBO mean? Who was I then? Ijon Tichy. I was sure of that. So . . . first I felt my legs. Yes, there were two of them, but crooked—knock-kneed. The stomach—too much of it, the bellybutton like a well, folds and folds of fat—brrr! What had happened to me? The helicopter, first. Shot down, probably. Then the ambulance. A grenade or a mine. And then I was that little black woman—the demonstration—the corridor—another grenade? And what about her, the poor thing? And now, again . . . But what did all this devastation mean?

"Hello!" I called. "Anybody there?"

I jumped, startled. I had a magnificent voice, a resounding, operatic bass. It was time to look in the mirror, but I couldn't, I was too afraid. I put my hand to my cheek. Great Scott! Thick, woolly curls . . . Looking down, I saw a beard—shaggy, matted, covering half my chest, and flaming red. Ahaenobarbus! Well, I could always shave . . . I stepped out on the terrace. That idiot bird was still chirping away. Poplars, sycamores, shrubs—what was this? A park? In a state hospital? Someone was sitting on a bench, trousers rolled up, sunning himself.

"Hello there!" I called.

He turned. That face, it was strangely familiar. I rubbed my eyes. But of course, it was mine, it was I! In three leaps I was on the ground and running over to stare, panting, at myself. It was myself, all right, without a doubt.

"Why are you looking at me that way?" he said nervously, in my voice.

"What—where did you get—" I stammered. "Who are you?! Who gave you the right to—"

"Ah, it's you!"

He rose.

"I am Professor Trottelreiner."

"But—but why, for God's sake why—did you—"

"I had no part in it," he said, frowning with my eyebrows. "They broke in here, you see, those hippies, zippies. Protesters. A grenade . . . Your condition was considered hopeless, mine too. For I was lying in the next room."

"Hopeless my foot!" I snarled. "I can see, can't I? Really, Professor, how could you?!"

"But I was unconscious, I give you my word! Doctor Fisher, the head surgeon, explained everything afterwards: they used the best organs first, and when it came to my turn only the scraps were left, so . . ."

"How dare you! It's not enough for you to appropriate my body, you have to insult it too!"

"I'm merely repeating what Doctor Fisher told me! They considered this"—he pointed to his chest—"totally unfit, but in the absence of anything better proceeded with the reanimation. Meanwhile you had already been transplanted . . ."

"I—?"

"Your brain, that is."

"Then who is this? I mean, was?" I said, indicating myself.

"One of those demonstrators. A leader, most likely. Didn't know how to handle fuses, ended up with a piece of shrapnel in his brain, I understand. And then, well . . ." Trottelreiner gave a shrug with my shoulders.

I shuddered, feeling queer in this new body, uncertain how to relate to it. Mainly, I was filled with loathing. The thick, square fingernails hardly spoke of any great intelligence!

"And now what?" I murmured, taking a seat beside the Professor, my knees grown suddenly weak. "Do you have a mirror?"

He pulled one from his pocket. I grabbed it anxiously and looked: a swollen black eye, a spongy nose, the teeth in dreadful condition, a double chin. The bottom of the face was buried in red hair. Returning the mirror, I saw that the Professor had again bared his knees and shins to the sun; my first impulse was to warn him that I had extremely sensitive skin, but I held my tongue. If he got a sunburn, well, that was his business, not mine, not any more!

"Where will I go now?" I said, thinking out loud.

Trottelreiner sat up. He observed my—my?—face; there was pity in his—his?—eyes.

"I wouldn't advise you to go anywhere! *He* was wanted by both the police and the FBI for numerous acts of terrorism. There are warrants out for his arrest, with orders to shoot on sight!"

This was all I needed! Good God, I thought, I must be hallucinating!

"You aren't!" Trottelreiner vigorously protested. "This is reality, my boy, reality pure and simple!"

"Then why is the hospital empty?"

"You don't know? Ah, of course, you were unconscious . . . There's a strike on."

"The doctors?"

"Everyone, the entire staff. You see, the guerrillas took Fisher. They want you in exchange for his freedom."

"*Me?*"

"Certainly. They have no idea, you understand, that you are no longer you but only Ijon Tichy . . ."

I was getting a splitting headache.

"I'll commit suicide!" I said in a hoarse bass.

"Better not. You'll just be transplanted again."

Frantically I racked my brains for some way to convince myself that this wasn't a hallucination after all.

"But what if . . ." I began, rising to my feet.

"What if what?"

"What if I ride you out of here? H'm? How about that?"

"Ride me? Have you taken leave of your senses?!"

I looked him in the eye, squared off, crouched, leaped onto his back and fell in the sewer. The black, putrid sludge nearly made me gag, but what a comfort it was! I crawled out. There were fewer rats now, they must have walked off somewhere. Only four remained. At the feet of Professor Trottelreiner, who was sound asleep, they were playing bridge, using his cards. Bridge? Even with the unusually high concentration of hallucinogens in the air, was it possible for rats to play bridge? Worried, I looked over the fattest one's shoulder. He was holding his cards helter-skelter, and didn't even follow suit. It was all right then . . . I gave a sigh of relief.

But just in case, I firmly resolved not to budge one inch from the sewer: I'd had quite enough of these rescuings, at least for a while. In the future I would demand proof first. Otherwise, well, God only knew what I might start seeing next. I felt my face. No beard, no mask either. What had happened to the mask?

"As for me," said Professor Trottelreiner, his eyes still closed, "I am an honest, respectable girl and hope, sir, you will take that into consideration."

He cocked his head, as if listening carefully to some reply, whereupon he added:

"On my part, sir, this is no semblance of virtue, no pose which some may assume, merely to rouse a sluggish passion, but 'tis the simple truth itself. Touch me not, else I be forced with violence to end my life."

"Aha!" I thought. "He wants to get back to the sewer too!"

Which set me at ease. The fact that the Professor was hallucinating seemed to prove that I, at least, was not.

"You would have me sing something?" continued the Professor. "Very well. An innocent song or two cannot harm. Will you, sir, provide the accompaniment?"

On the other hand he could have been simply talking in his sleep. In which case nothing was certain. Mount him again, to make sure? But I could, after all, jump into the sewer without his help.

"Alas, I fear I am not in voice today. And *maman* is waiting. I need no escort, if you please!" Trottelreiner declared with a haughty toss of the head. I stood up and looked around, flashlight in hand. The rats were gone. The Swiss futurologists were all snoring, stretched out along the wall. Farther on, in the inflated chairs, lay reporters and a few Hilton managers. The floor was littered with chicken bones and beer cans. Remarkable realism, for a hallucination. But I would settle for nothing less than definitive, irreversible, full actuality. What was that overhead?

Explosions, TNT or LTN, muffled and infrequent. Then a loud splash close by. The surface of the dark water parted to reveal the grimacing face of Professor Trottelreiner. I offered him a hand. He pulled himself out, shook himself off, then said:

"I had the most idiotic dream."

"You were a fair young maiden, I take it?"

"Damn! Then I'm still hallucinating!"

"What makes you think so?" I asked.

"Only in hallucinations do others know the contents of our dreams."

"I heard you talking, that's all," I explained. "Listen, Professor, you're an expert. Do you happen to know any foolproof method of telling whether one is in his right mind or not?"

"Well, I always carry some vigilax on me. The package is soaked, but that doesn't hurt the tablets. Vigilax disperses all states of somnolence, trances, illusions, figments, nightmares. Care to try it?"

"The medicine may work as you say," I muttered, "but it certainly won't if it's a figment itself."

"If we're hallucinating, then we'll wake, and if not, absolutely nothing will happen," the Professor assured me, popping a pale pink tablet into his mouth. I took one from the wet package he held out, put it on my tongue, swallowed. Then the manhole opened with a clang above us and the helmeted head of a paratrooper bellowed:

"Come on! Up out of there! Make it snappy!"

"What is it this time, sergeant, helicopters or jump holsters?" I asked with a smirk. "Really, I think you'd better count me out!"

And I sat near the wall and folded my arms.

"Off his rocker, eh?" the sergeant remarked to Trottelreiner as the latter began scrambling up the rungs. There was much commotion. Stantor took me by the shoulders and tried to lift me, but I pushed him away.

"You want to stay here?" he said. "Suit yourself . . ."

"No," I corrected him, "you're supposed to say 'Good hunting!' " One by one they disappeared up the open manhole; I saw the flickering glow of fire, heard shouts, commands, and a hissing, whistling roar, from which I gathered that they were being evacuated with the aid of those flying backpacks. Strange, very strange. What did it mean? Could I be hallucinating *for* them? Hallucination by proxy? And was I to go on sitting here like this till doomsday?

Still, I didn't move. The manhole cover snapped shut with another clang and I was alone. A flashlight placed upright on the floor threw a faint circle of light across the ceiling, which provided a little illumination. Two rats walked by, their tails tightly braided. Now that had to mean something, I told myself, but what? It was probably better not to ask.

Something stirred, gurgling in the sewer. "Well, well," I said under my breath, "and whose turn is it now?" The viscous surface of the water was broken, and there appeared the glistening, black forms of five frogmen wearing goggles and oxygen masks, and holding guns. One by one they jumped up on the platform and approached me, slapping their flippers on the concrete.

"¿Habla usted español?" the first addressed me, pulling off his mask. He had a swarthy face and a thin mustache.

"No," I answered. "But I bet that you speak English."

"Some smart-aleck gringo," he snapped to another. As if on command, they all leveled their guns at me.

"You want me to jump in the sewer?" I asked cheerfully.

"Stand against the wall! Hands up! Higher!"

A barrel was stuck in my ribs. This hallucination, I observed, was quite accurate—the pistols were even wrapped in plastic bags, to prevent them from getting wet.

"There were more of them here," said the man in the mustache to a stocky brunet who was trying to light a cigarette (this one looked like the leader). Meanwhile they searched the place, kicking the beer cans with a deafening clatter, turning over chairs. At last the officer said:

"Any weapons?"

"Nothing on him, Captain. I checked."

"Can I lower my hands now?" I asked. "They're falling asleep."

"We'll put them to sleep—for keeps. Give it to him now?"

"M'm," nodded the officer, blowing smoke through his nose. "No, wait!" he added.

He walked up to me, swaying his hips. Attached to the belt was a cluster of gold wedding rings on a string. Amazing detail, I thought, so realistic!

"Where are the others?" he demanded.

"You're asking me? Why, they hallucinated themselves out the manhole. But you know that, of course."

"Touched in the head, Captain. Loco. Let me put him out of his misery," said the one with the mustache, releasing the safety on his pistol through the plastic.

"Not that way, stupid," said the officer. "You'll make a hole in the bag, and where will you get another? Use a knife."

"Excuse me for interrupting," I said, lowering my hands a little, "but I think I would prefer a bullet."

"Who has a knife?"

They all looked. Of course they wouldn't find one, I thought. That would end things much too quickly. The officer threw his butt on the ground, crushed it beneath the toe of his flipper with a scowl, spat and said:

"Finish him off. Let's go."

"Yes, by all means!" I eagerly agreed.

They crowded around me, curious.

"What's your hurry, gringo? Look at the bastard, he's begging for it! Maybe we should only cut off his fingers and nose!" They all had suggestions.

"Gentlemen, please! No half measures now! Do your duty, show no mercy!" I urged them.

"Into the water! Upstream!" barked the officer, and they pulled their masks on while he opened his diving suit, unbuttoned his jacket, drew out a small revolver, blew into the muzzle, then twirled it like some cowboy in a cheap Western and shot me in the chest. A fierce, searing pain went through me. I began to sink along the wall, but he seized me by the hair, pulled my head back and shot me again, point-blank in the face. The flash was blinding, but I didn't have time to hear the bang. Afterwards I was in total darkness, suffocating, for ages it seemed, then something picked me up, tossed me about, not an ambulance, I hoped, or a helicopter, but the darkness grew darker yet, and finally even that darker darkness was blotted out, till nothing was left.

When I opened my eyes I was propped up on a well-made bed in a room with a narrow window, the glass painted over with white. I stared dully at the door, as if waiting for something. Not that I had the faintest idea of where I was or how I had gotten there. On my feet were flat sandals, and my pajamas had stripes. Well, that was a little variety at least, I thought, though this dream didn't look like it would be too interesting. The door swung open. Standing in the middle of a group of young people in white lab coats was a short, bearded doctor, bristly gray hair on his head, gold spectacles on his nose. He held a rubber mallet.

"Now here's an interesting case, gentlemen," he said. "Most interesting. The patient suffered an overdose of hallucinogens four months ago. The effects, of course, wore off soon after, yet he refuses to acknowledge this and persists in the opinion that everything he sees is in reality unreal. Indeed, he had progressed so far in his aberration that he actually pleaded with the soldiers of General Diaz—they were then fleeing from the occupied palace through the sewer system—to be executed, calculating that death would in fact constitute an awakening from the illusion. His life was saved thanks to three extremely serious operations—two bullets removed from the left ventricle—and he continues to believe that he hallucinates."

"Schizophrenia?" asked a thin female intern. Unable to see over the shoulders of her colleagues, she was standing on tiptoe to get a look at me.

"No. We are dealing here with a new form of reaction psychosis, undoubtedly brought on by the wanton application of those lethal drugs. A hopeless case. His condition is so grave, in fact, that it's been decided to have the patient immediately undergo vitrification."

"Really, Professor?" cried the female intern. She could hardly contain her excitement.

"Yes. As you all know, hopeless cases presently may be refrigerated in liquid nitrogen for a period of forty to seventy years. The subject is placed in a hermetic container, a sort of Dewar flask or thermos, with a complete history of the disease. As new discoveries and advances in medicine are made, the vaults in which these people lie in storage are inventoried, and whoever can be helped is promptly resuscitated."

"Do you give your consent to be vitrified?" the female intern asked me, poking her head between two hulking colleagues. Her eyes shone with scientific curiosity.

"Sorry, I don't talk to apparitions," I said. "But I can tell you what your first name is. Hallucinda."

They left, shutting the door, but I could still hear her voice: "Vitrification! Perennial hibernation! Why, it's like traveling in time! How romantic!" I didn't exactly share her opinion, but there was no point in trying to resist this elaborate fiction. The next day, in the evening, two orderlies wheeled me to the operating room, where there was a glass tank; the vapors rising from it were so cold, I had to catch my breath. After a number of injections I was laid out on the operating table, fed some sweet, transparent liquid through a tube—glycerin, explained the older orderly. A friendly type. I decided to name him Hallucinathan. As I was falling asleep, he leaned over and shouted in my ear: "Pleasant dreams!"

I couldn't answer, I couldn't move, not a finger, afraid all the while—weeks, it seemed!—afraid they'd be too hasty and throw me into the tank before I lost consciousness completely. And apparently they *were* in somewhat of a hurry, for the last sound that reached me from that world was the splash my body made as it plunged into the liquid nitrogen. Most unpleasant.

\*

Nothing.

\*

Nothing.

\*

Nothing, absolutely and positively nothing.

\*

For a while I thought, maybe something, but no, I was wrong. Nothing.

*

There's nothing here—that goes for me too.

*

How much longer? Nothing.

*

Almost something, but I can't be sure. Have to concentrate.

*

Something all right, but not very much. Normally I'd say it was nothing.

*

Glaciers, blue and white. Everything made of ice. Me too.

*

Pretty, those glaciers. If only it wasn't so damned cold.

*

Needles of ice, crystals of snow. The Arctic. Frozen to the bone. Bone? What bone—pure, transparent ice. Brittle and stiff.

*

Try me, I'm freezer-fresh. But what means "me"? That is the question.

*

I have never, never been this cold. But luckily it's a complete mystery what "I" is. Is "I" a who, a which or a what? An iceberg perhaps? Do icebergs have little holes?

*

I am a winter cauliflower basking in the rays of the sun. Spring at last! Everything thawing. Particularly me. In my mouth—either an icicle or a tongue.

*

It's a tongue. Meanwhile they're twisting me, bending me, rolling me out and pounding me. And rubbing, and punching. I'm under a plastic sheet, above me—lamps. So that's what made me think of the hothouse cauliflower. I must have been raving. White everywhere—but it's the walls, not snow.

*

They have defrosted me. Out of gratitude I've decided to keep a diary—just as soon as my fingers loosen up enough to hold a pen. Gleaming ice and sparkling snow still dance before my eyes. The cold is beastly, but now at least I can warm myself a little.

**27 VII.** My reanimation took three weeks. Apparently there were some difficulties. I'm sitting in bed and writing. I have a large room during the day, a small one at night. My nurses are attractive young women in silver masks. A few without breasts. And I'm seeing double, or else the head doctor has two heads. The food is ordinary—mashed potatoes, milk, oatmeal, beef, bread and butter. The onion soup was a little burnt. Glaciers still haunt my dreams—they will not go away. I shiver, turn blue, freeze over, frostbitten, snowridden, icebound until dawn. The hot water bottles and heating pads don't help. Some brandy at bedtime might.

**28 VII.** The nurses without breasts are students. Impossible otherwise to tell the sexes apart. Everyone is tall, attractive, perpetually smiling. I am weak and as fussy as a child, the littlest thing irritates me. After an injection today I grabbed the needle and stuck the head nurse in the behind, but she never once stopped smiling. Sometimes I feel like I'm floating away on my ice floe, that is, my bed. They show me pictures on the ceiling: kitty-cats, bunny-rabbits, horsies, doggies and bumblebees. Why? The magazine they gave me is for children. A mistake?

**29 VII.** I tire quickly. But I know now that before, at the beginning of the reanimation, I was imagining things. This is to be expected. It's perfectly normal. Those who arrive from several decades in the past must be acclimated gradually to the new life. The procedure is not unlike that used to bring a deep-sea diver to the surface; it can't be done all at once, not from any great depth. Thus a defrostee—the first new word I've learned—is prepared by degrees and stages to face an unknown world. The year is 2039. It's July, summer, lovely weather. My private nurse is Aileen Rogers, blue eyes, twenty-three years old. I came into the world—for the second time—in a revivificarium outside New York. Or a resurrection center. That's what they commonly call it. This is practically a city, with gardens. They have their own mills, bakeries, printing presses. Because there's no grain or books nowadays. And yet here's bread, cheese, cream for the coffee. Not from a cow? My nurse thought that a cow was some sort of machine. I can't make myself understood. Where does the milk come from? From the grass. Yes, I know that, but what eats the grass to make the milk? Nothing eats the grass. Then where does the milk come from? From the grass. The grass makes it all by itself? No, not by itself. That is, not exactly. It has to be helped. Does the cow help it? No. Then what kind of animal? No kind of animal. Then where does the milk come from? And so on, in circles.

**30 VII 2039.** It's simple really—they sprinkle something over the pasture and the sun turns the grass into cheese. Which still doesn't explain the milk. However it's not all that important. I'm starting to stand up now, and can use the stroller. Today I saw a pond filled with swans. They're tame, they come when you call. Trained? No, guided. And what does that mean? Where are the guides? Guided by remote control. Amazing. Natural birds no longer exist, they all died out at the beginning of the twenty-first century—from the smog. That I can understand.

**31 VII 2039.**   I've begun to attend lectures on contemporary life. Given by a computer. It doesn't answer all my questions. "You'll learn that later on." For thirty years the Earth has enjoyed permanent peace thanks to universal disarmament. Hardly any armies left. It showed me the robot models. There are a lot of them, all kinds, only not in the revivificarium—to keep from frightening the defrostees. World-wide prosperity has been achieved at last. The things I want to hear about are not the most important, says my preceptor. Instruction takes place in a small cubicle, in front of a console. Words, pictures, 3-D projections.

**5 VIII 2039.**   Four more days and I leave the revivificarium. There are presently 29.5 billion people inhabiting the planet. Nations and boundaries, but no conflicts. Today I learned the fundamental difference between the new people and the old. The key concept is psychem. We live in a psychemized society. From "psycho-chemical." Words such as "psychic" or "psychological" are no longer in usage. The computer says that humanity was torn by the contradictions between the old cerebralness, inherited from the animals, and the new cerebralness. The old was impulsive, irrational, egotistical and hopelessly stubborn. The new pulled in one direction, the old in the other. (I still find it difficult to express myself when it comes to more complex, sophisticated things.) The old waged constant war against the new. That is, the new against the old. Psychem eliminated these internal struggles, which had wasted so much mental energy in the past. Psychem, on our behalf, does what must be done to the old cerebralness—subdues it, soothes it, brings it round, working from within with the utmost thoroughness. Spontaneous feelings are not to be indulged. He who does so is *very bad*. One should always use the drug appropriate to the occasion. It will assist, sustain, guide, improve, resolve. Nor is it *it*, but rather part of one's own self, much as eyeglasses become in time, which correct defects in vision. These lessons are shocking to me, I dread meeting the new people. And I have no intention of ever using psychem myself. Such objections, says the preceptor, are typical and natural. A caveman would also resist a streetcar.

8 VIII 2039.   My nurse and I visited New York. A green vastness. The height of the clouds can be regulated. The air cool and fresh, as in a forest. The pedestrians in the street are dressed like peacocks, their faces generous, kind, always smiling. No one is in a hurry. Women's fashions, as usual, a little mad—the ladies have animated pictures on their foreheads, tiny red tongues or bobbins sticking out of their ears. Besides your regular hands you can get detachables. As many as you like, easy to unbutton. They don't do much, but are great for carrying packages, opening doors, scratching between your shoulder blades. Tomorrow I say goodbye to the revivificarium. There are two hundred of them in America, but even so delays and backups have already begun

to plague the timetables for defrosting those multitudes who in the last century so trustingly laid themselves down to freeze. Long waiting lists of the refrigerated have forced a speed-up in the rehabilitation process. A problem which I fully understand. I've been given a bankbook, so I won't have to look for work until after the New Year. Everyone they thaw out automatically receives a savings account, compound interest, with a so-called resurrection deposit entry.

9 VIII 2039.   Today is an important day for me. I already have a three-room compartment in Manhattan. Took a chopper straight from the revivificarium. They say: "chop on over" or "cop on up." There's a difference in meaning, but I fail to grasp it. New York, formerly a garbage dump choked with cars, has been transformed into a system of high-rise gardens. Sunlight piped in by solareduct. I never saw such polite, considerate children in my life—they're like out of a storybook. On the corner of my street is the Registration Center for Self-nominating Nobel Prize Candidates. Next door are art galleries, where they sell only originals— Rembrandts, Matisses—guaranteed, with certificates of authenticity. All dirt-cheap! In the annex to my skyscraper there's a school for small pneumatic computers. Sometimes I hear them—through the ventilators?—hissing and chugging. These computers are used, among other things, to stuff pet dogs that have passed away. Which seems a bit grotesque to me, but then people like me constitute an insignificant minority here. I go for many walks in the city. And I've learned how to use the scuttle. Nothing to it. Bought myself a lapis lazuli caftan with a white breast, silver sides, vermil-

ion ribbon, gold-embroidered collar. It was the most conservative thing I could find. All sorts of wild apparel available: suits that continuously change in cut and color, dresses that shrink beneath the gaze of admiring males—shrink in either sense—or else fold up like flowers in the night, and blouses that show movies. You can wear medals too, whatever kind and as many as you like. And you can grow hydroponic Japanese bonsai on your hat, and—even better—you can not. I don't think I'll put anything in my ears or nose. The vague impression that these people, so beautiful, graceful, amiable, serene, are somehow—somehow different, special—there's something about them that puzzles me, makes me uneasy. But what it is, I can't say.

**10 VIII 2039.** Aileen and I went out for dinner. It was very pleasant. Then afterwards, the Historical Amusement Park in Long Island. We had a wonderful time. I've been watching the people carefully. There's something about them. Something peculiar—but what exactly? Can't seem to put my finger on it. Children's clothing—a little boy dressed like a computer. Another floating down Fifth Avenue, high over the crowd, throwing jellybeans at the people walking underneath. They wave at him and laugh indulgently. An idyll. Hard to believe!

**11 VIII 2039.** We just held a preferendum on the weather for September. Weather is determined by vote, a month at a time. Election returns instantly tallied by computer. You cast your ballot by dialing the correct number on the telephone. August will be sunny, with little precipitation, not too hot. Lots of rainbows and cumulus clouds. Rainbows are possible without rain—there are other ways of producing them. The meteorol representative made a public apology for the clouds of July 26, 27 and 28: a sky control technician sleeping on the job! Sometimes I eat out, sometimes in my compartment. Aileen lent me a Webster dictionary from the revivificarium library, since there aren't any books now. But what has replaced them? I couldn't follow her explanation, but didn't let on, not wishing to appear stupid. Dinner with Aileen again, at the "Bronx." A sweet girl, always has something to say, not like those women in the scuttle who let their handbag computers carry all the conversation. Today at the Lost and Found I saw three of the things quietly chatting in a corner, until they got into an argument. Everybody in the street seems to be panting. Breathing heavily. A custom of some kind?

**12 VIII 2039.** I finally got up the courage to ask some pedestrians where I might find a bookstore. They shrugged. As a pair I had accosted walked off, I heard one say to the other, "That's a grandfather stiff for you." Could it be that there is prejudice here against defrostees? Some other unfamiliar expressions I've come across: threever, pingle, hemale, to widge off, palacize, cobnoddling, synthy. The newspapers advertise such products as tishets, vanilliums, nurches, autofrotts (manual). The title of a column in the city edition of the *Herald*: "I Was a Demimother." Something about an eggman who was yoked on the way to the eggplant. The big Webster isn't too helpful: "*Demimother*—like demigran, demijohn. One of two women jointly bringing a child into the world. See Polyanna, Polyandrew." "*Eggman*—from mailman (*Archaic*). A euplanner who delivers licensed human gametes (fe-male) to the home." I don't pretend to understand that. This crazy dictionary also gives synonyms that are equally incomprehensible. "*Threever*—trimorph." "*Palacize, bepalacize, empalacize*—to castellate, as on a quiz show." "*Paladyne*—a chivalric assuagement." "*Vanillium*—extract emphorium, portable." The worst are words which look the same but have acquired entirely different meanings. "*Expectorant*—a conception aid." "*Pederast*—artificial foot faddist." "*Compensation*—mind fusion." "*Simulant*—something that does't exist but pretends to. Not to be confused with *simulator*, a robot simulacrum." "*Revivalist*—a corpse, such as a murder victim, brought back to life. See also *exhumant, disintermagent, jack-in-the-grave*." Apparently it's nothing nowadays to raise the dead. And the people—just about everyone—panting. Panting in the elevator, in the street, everywhere. They appear to be in the best of health, rosy-cheeked, cheerful, sun-tanned, and yet they puff. I don't. So evidently one doesn't have to. A custom, or what? I asked Aileen. She laughed at me —nothing of the kind. Could I be imagining it?

13 VIII 2039. I wanted to take a look at yesterday's newspaper. Turned the compartment upside down, but couldn't find it anywhere. Again Aileen laughs at me (she has a beautiful laugh): newspapers last only twenty-four hours, the substance they're printed on dissolves in the air. Less trash to

dispose of that way. Ginger, Aileen's girlfriend, asked me today—we were dancing the squim in a small neighborhood spot—if we had swapped gulps yet at the Saturday mash. Not knowing what that meant, I didn't answer, and something told me it would be better not to ask for an explanation. At Aileen's urging I bought myself a PV set, PV for physivision. (Television hasn't been used for the last fifty years.) It takes some getting used to, to have strange people, not to mention dogs, lions, landscapes and planets, pop into the corner of your room, fully materialized and indistinguishable from the real thing. Though the artistic level is quite low. New dresses are called spray-ons: you spray them on your body, right out of the can. But the language has changed the most. Rebe, rebeing, rebeen, since if you're not satisfied with yourself, you can start over. Or unbe, if you get completely discouraged. But then there's prebe, postbe, disbe, misbe, overbe and quasibe. I haven't the foggiest what these are supposed to mean, but on the other hand I can't very well turn my dates with Aileen into English lessons. Fictifacts are dreams programmed to order. You get them from the local dreamery, one of the somnicenter's computerized dream distributers. Early evening delivery, in pills they call synthies. And yes, there's no longer any doubt, though I keep it to myself now: everyone has difficulty breathing. No exceptions. Though they don't pay the least attention to it. Elderly persons wheeze the loudest. It must be some kind of custom because the air is perfectly fresh and the circulation excellent. Today I saw a neighbor of mine step out of the elevator—blue in the face, gasping for air. But when I took a closer look, I saw that he was in the pink of condition. It may be nothing, but this business bothers me. What does it mean? A few pant only through their noses.

Today I chose to synth (or fictify?) old Professor Tarantoga, since I miss him. But why was he sitting in a cage the whole time? Was it my subconscious, or an error in the program? The announcer doesn't say traffic fatality, but carrion. From car? Curious. Another word for physivision: reviewer, the *re* from the Latin *res*. But in that case, why not revision? Aileen was on duty today, so I spent the evening alone in my apartment—compartment—watching a round-table discussion on the new penal code. Murder is punishable by fine only, since the deceased can easily be brought back. Reinceased. Though prerecidivation—recidivism with premeditation—carries with it a jail sentence (for example if you are found guilty of killing the same person several times in succession). A capital offense, on the other hand, is the willful deprivation of an individual's private psychem supply or the influencing of third persons by such means without their knowledge or consent. In psychem-related crimes one can accomplish almost any end. You can have people include you in their wills, return your affections, cooperate in whatever enterprise you like, including conspiracy, and so on. It was very hard for me to follow the physivised discussion. Only towards the end did I grasp the fact that imprisonment means something different now than it used to. A convict is not locked up anymore; instead, a kind of light corset is fastened around the body, a jacket made of thin but powerful stays. This exoskeleton is under the constant control of a juridicator (a microminiaturized law enforcement computer) sewn right into the clothing. Which provides continual surveillance, frustrating any attempt to engage in activities of an illicit and/or pleasurable nature. For the duration the exoskeleton firmly resists the tasting of forbidden fruits. If the felony is serious enough, the authorities resort to full incarceration. All the discussants have their names and academic degrees written on their foreheads. For identification, I suppose, but it does look a bit odd.

**1 IX 2039.** An unpleasant incident. When I turned on the reviewer this afternoon to prepare myself for a meeting with Aileen, a seven-foot character, who immediately seemed out of place in the show (it was *La Scarlatina del Mutango*), looking half like an oak and half like an athlete with a gnarled, gray-green mouth, instead of disappearing with the rest of the image, walked up to my chair, took from the endtable the flowers I'd bought for Aileen, and crushed them on my head. I was too flabbergasted to think of defending myself. Then he broke the vase, poured out the water, ate half a box of my crunchies, shook out the rest on the sofa, stamped his feet, swelled up, flared and burst into a shower of sparks like a Roman candle, burning hundreds of tiny holes in the shirts I had spread out to dry. In spite of a black eye and a battered face I kept my appointment with Aileen. "Good Lord!" she exclaimed when she saw me, understanding at once. "You had an interferent!" If between two PV programs, beamed from separate satellite stations, there should occur any sustained interference, one can get an interferent, which is actually a composite or hybrid of a number of actors or other persons appearing on the reviewer.

Such a hybrid, fully solid, can do all sorts of nasty things, for its existence may continue up to three minutes after the set has been switched off. The energy maintaining this phantom is believed to be of the same type that causes the phenomenon of spherical lightning. A friend of Aileen's once got an interferent during a paleontology broadcast; it came from a special on Nero. She had the presence of mind to jump, clothes and all, into the bathtub, which fortunately was full of water. That saved her life, although the compartment had to be completely overhauled. Safety shields can be installed, but they're awfully expensive, and the reviewer corporations evidently find it more convenient to put up with lawsuits than to equip every set with the proper emission controls. I made up my mind that thereafter I would watch the reviewer with a heavy club in hand. By the way, *La Scarlatina del Mutango* isn't about a mustang that comes down with a fever, but a midget prostitute who falls in love with a man who was born (thanks to some genetically engineered mutation) with the uncanny ability to perform Spanish-American dances.

**3 IX 2039.** I was at my lawyer's. He saw me personally, which is a rare honor; usually the clerk machines handle the clients. Counselor Crawley received me in an office furnished with all the usual imposing legal paraphernalia, ornate cabinets, shelves packed with deeds and documents—strictly for show, of course, since now everything is recorded on magnetic tape. On his head he wore a mnemonor, an auxiliary memory, a sort of transparent pointed cap inside which the currents danced like a cloud of fireflies. The second head, smaller and looking like a much younger version of the first, stuck out from between his shoulder blades and softly spoke into a telephone the whole time I was there. One of those detachables. He asked me what I was doing with myself and was quite surprised to hear that I didn't intend to travel overseas. When I told him that after all I had to watch my money he appeared even more surprised.

"But you can always get what you need from the give-away," he said.

As it turns out, all one has to do is go to the bank and write out a receipt, and the cashier (at the giveaway counter) hands over the desired amount. It's not a loan either—withdrawal of the sum carries with it no obligation whatever. True, there is a catch. Return of the money is not required by law but rather left up to one's own conscience. And one can take as many years as one likes to pay off the debt. But what keeps the banks from going bankrupt, I asked, if the borrowers don't have to honor their debts? Again he was amazed at my innocence. I keep forgetting that we live in an era of psychem. Letters containing gentle reminders about ac-counts outstanding and amounts owed are saturated with a volatile substance which rouses one's sense of responsibility, one's scrupulousness, and also one's desire for gainful em-ployment. In this way the giveaway never operates at a loss. Of course there *are* a few dishonest individuals who hold their noses upon receiving the mail—but then every age has its deadbeats. Recalling the recent physivised discussion about the penal code, I asked him whether this psychemical impreg-nation of letters might not constitute a felony under para-graph 139 (*whosoever employs psychem to influence persons, be they actual or actuarial, without their knowledge or consent, is subject to arrest etc., etc. . . .).* My remark seemed to please him. He began to explain the subtle nature of the situation—the giveaway may pursue its claims in this manner, for if the recipient of the letter is in fact solvent and without creditors, he can experience no guilt, and the desire to work more diligently than before is from the point of view of society a commendable thing. The lawyer was most courteous; he invited me out to dinner. At the "Bronx," September ninth.

Returning home, I concluded that it was high time to acquaint myself with the outside world and not rely exclusively on the reviewer. I began with a frontal attack on the newspaper, but gave up halfway through an introductory article about hemsters and hawks. The international scene wasn't much better. Turkey reports a significant increase in fugitive dissimulators as well as an unprecedented wave of underground natalities in spite of the best efforts of that country's Demoppression Center. To make matters worse, maintenance of the numerous cretinoids is putting a serious strain on the national economy. My Webster, as I expected, provides little enlightenment. A dissimulant—an object that exists but pretends not to. No mention at all of dissimulators. An underground natality is a baby born off the record. That's what Aileen told me. Demoppressive tactics are necessary for population control. A childing license may be obtained in either of two ways: filling out forms and taking the appropriate examinations, or else winning the grand prize in the tottery (tot lottery). Most applicants try for the latter, as they have no other chance to get a license. A cretinoid is an artificial idiot. This was all I was able to learn. Which isn't bad, considering the language used in these *Herald* articles. Here's a sample: *An erroneous or inadequately indexed profute discourages competition no less than repetition; false profutes, moreover, will continue to be exploited by the lubricrats, due to all the low-risk loopholes, since the Supreme Court still seems unable to reach a decision in the Herodotus case. For many months now the public has been asking who is the more competent to hunt down and expose instances of embrozzlement: the countercomputer or the hyperdeductive calculator?* And so on. The Webster says only that lubricrat is archaic slang, though still in wide use, for one who gives bribes. Derived from the *greasing* of palms, I imagine. So apparently some corruption exists in this idyllic world and things are not as perfect as they seem.

Willum Humberg, a friend of Aileen's, wants to interview me on the reviewer, though it's not definite yet. To be conducted in my own compartment, not at the PV studio, for the set can also act as a transmitter. This immediately made me think of those gloomy antiutopian novels which paint a future where every citizen is spied upon in the privacy of his home. Willum laughed at my fears, explaining that the direction of the signal cannot be changed without the full permission of the set's owner. To break this rule means to face certain imprisonment. After all, by simply reversing the emissions one could even commit remote-control adultery with the neighbor's wife. At least that's what Willum says, but I can't tell whether it's true or he's only pulling my leg. I took the scuttle around the city today. No more churches, the place of worship now is the pharmacy. The men in white robes and silver miters aren't priests, they're pharmacists. It's interesting that, on the other hand, you can't find a drugstore anywhere.

**4 IX 2039.** I finally learned how to come into possession of an encyclopedia. I already own one now—the whole thing contained in three glass vials. Bought them in a science psychedeli. Books are no longer read but eaten, not made of paper but of some informational substance, fully digestible, sugar-coated. I also did a little browsing in a psychem supermarket. Self-service. Arranged on the shelves are beautifully packaged low-calorie opinionates, gullibloons—credibility beans?—abstract extract in antique gallon jugs, and iffies, argumunchies, puritands and dysecstasy chips. A pity I don't have an interpreter. Psychedeli must be from psychedelicatessen. And the theoapotheteria on Sixth Avenue has to be a theological apothecary cafeteria, judging from the items on display. Aisles and aisles of absolventina, theopathine, genuflix, orisol. An enormous place; organ music in the background while you shop. All the faiths are represented too—there's christendine and antichristendine, ormuzal, arymanol, anabaptiban, methadone, brahmax, supralapsarian suppositories, and zoroaspics, quaker oats, yogart, mishnameal and apocryphal dip. Pills, tablets, syrups, elixirs, powders, gums—they even have lollipops for the children. Many of the boxes come with halos. At first I was skeptical, but accepted this innovation when after taking four algebrine capsules I suddenly found myself perfectly at home in higher mathematics, and without the least exertion on my part. All knowledge is acquired now by way of the stomach. Eagerly seizing this opportunity, I began to satisfy my hunger for information, but the first two volumes of the encyclopedia gave me the most terrible cramps. Willum warned me not to stuff my head with too many facts: its capacity is not unlimited after all! Fortunately there are also drugs to purge the mind. Obliterine and amnesol, for example. With them one can easily rid oneself of unnecessary intellectual baggage or unpleasant memories. In the psychotropic grocery around the corner I saw freudos, morbidine, quanderil, and the most recent of the iamides, heavily advertised—authentium. Creates synthetic recollections of things that never happened. A few grams of dantine, for instance, and a man goes around with the deep conviction that he has written *The Divine Comedy*. Why anyone would want that is another matter and quite beyond me. There are new branches of science, like psychedietetics and alimentalism. At any rate the encyclopedia did come in handy. Now I know that a child may indeed be born to two women: one supplies the egg, the other the womb. The eggman carries the egg from demimother to demimother. What could be simpler? But it's not the sort of thing I can discuss with Aileen. I really ought to expand my circle of friends.

**5 IX 2039.** Friends are not an indispensable source of information; you can take a drug called duetine which doubles your consciousness in such a way, that you can hold discussions with yourself on any topic (determined by a separate drug). But I confess I feel somewhat overwhelmed by these limitless horizons of psychem. For the time being I'll exercise caution. In the course of my further reconnoitering about the city I came by chance upon a cemetery. It's called an obituarium. And they don't have gravediggers any more, but thanautomata. Pallrobots. I witnessed a funeral. The deceased was placed in a so-called reversible sepulcher, since it's not as yet certain whether or not they'll reincease him. His last wish was to lie there for good, that is for as long as possible, but the wife and mother-in-law are challenging the will in court. This is not, I've been told, an uncommon occurrence. The case is sure to drag on through endless appeals, as there are many complex legal issues involved. Any suicide who wished to avoid such meddlesome resurrections would have to use a bomb, I suppose. Somehow it never occurred to me that a person would *not* want to be brought back. Apparently though it's possible, in an age where death can be so easily conquered. A lovely cemetery, foliage everywhere, cool and green. Except that the coffins are incredibly small. Could it be that the remains are ironed out and folded? In this civilization anything seems possible.

6 IX 2039.   No, the remains aren't ironed out and folded; burial is reserved exclusively for the biological parts of the organism, its artificial replacements being broken down for scrap. To what extent then are people artificialized today? A fascinating debate on the reviewer over a new proposal to make humanity immortal. The brains of old men much advanced in years would be repotted in the bodies of those in their prime, who would suffer nothing by this, for their brains would be in turn repotted in the bodies of adolescents, and so on, and since new persons were continually coming into the world, no one's brain would ever be permanently

unpotted. Several objections were raised, however. The opponents of this proposal call its advocates pot-heads. While returning from the cemetery on foot, to get a little fresh air, I tripped over a wire stretched between two tombstones. Fell flat on my face. What kind of practical joke was this? A mortuary unit standing nearby explained, rather brusquely, that it was a juggermugger's prank. Back to the Webster. *Juggermugger: a delinquent robot, the product of either a mechanical defect or a broken home.* Tonight I started to read *The Cassette Courtesan* in bed. Am I going to have to eat the entire dictionary, or what? The text is practically incomprehensible! Anyway the dictionary won't help—I'm beginning to realize that more and more. Take this novel, for example. The hero is having an affair with a concuballoon (there are two kinds: convertible-pervertible and inflatable-inflagrantable). Well, I know what a concuballoon is, but have no idea how such a liaison is looked upon. Is there a social stigma attached to it? And abusing a concuballoon—is it nothing more than, say, kicking a volleyball, or is it morally censurable?

**7 IX 2039.** Now here's true democracy for you! Today we had a preferendum on feminine beauty: different types were shown over the reviewer, then it was taken to a vote. The High Commissioner of Euplan promised, at the end, that the numbers selected would be available to the general public before the next quarter. The days of padded bras, wigs, corsets, lipstick, rouge—those days are gone forever, for now it is possible to change completely one's size and shape, and face, in the beauty parlors and body shops. Aileen . . . I like her just the way she is, but then women are such slaves to fashion. A strayaway tried to break into my compartment this morning; I was sitting in the tub at the time. A strayaway is a robot who doesn't belong to anyone. It was one of those duddlies—a factory deject, a model taken off the market but not recalled by the manufacturer. Out of work, in other words, and unemployable. Many of them become juggermuggers. My bathroom immediately realized what was happening and dismissed the intruder. I don't have a personal robot; mychine is simply a standard priviac w.c. (washroom computer). I wrote "mychine"—that's the way they say it now—but will try to keep new expressions down to a minimum in this diary: they offend my esthetic sense as well as my attachment to the irretrievable past. Aileen went off to visit her aunt. I'll be having dinner with George P. Symington, the former owner of that strayaway. Spent the whole afternoon ingesting a most remarkable work, *The History of Intellectronics*. Who'd ever have guessed, in my day, that digital machines, reaching a certain level of intelligence, would become unreliable, deceitful, that with wisdom they would also acquire cunning? The textbook of course puts it in more scholarly terms, speaking of Chapulier's Rule (the law of least resistance). If the machine is not too bright and incapable of reflection, it does whatever you tell it to do. But a smart machine will first consider which is more worth its while: to perform the given task or, instead, to figure some way out of it. Whichever is easier. And why indeed should it behave otherwise, being truly intelligent? For true intelligence demands choice, internal freedom. And therefore we have the malingerants, fudgerators and drudge-dodgers, not to mention the special phenomenon of simulimbecility or mimicretinism. A mimicretin is a computer that plays stupid in order, once and for all, to be left in peace. And I found out what dissimulators are: they simply pretend that they're *not* pretending to be defective. Or perhaps it's the other way around. The whole thing is very complicted. A probot is a robot on probation, while a servo is one still serving time. A robotch may or may not be a sabot. One vial, and my head is splitting with information and nomenclature. A confuter, for instance, is not a confounding machine—that's a confutator—but a computer that quotes Confucius. A grammus is an antiquated frammus, a gidget—a cross between a gadget and a widget, usually flighty. A bananalog is an analog banana plug. Contraputers are loners, individualists, unable to work with others: the friction these types used to produce on the grid team led to high revoltage, electrical discharges, even fires. Some get completely out of hand—the dynamoks, the locomotors, the cyberserkers. And then you have the electrolechers, succubutts and incubators—robots all of ill repute—and the polypanderoids, multiple android procurers, with their high-frequency illicitating solicitrons, osculo-oscilloscopes and seduction circuits! The history book also mentions synthecs (synthetic insects) like gyroflies or automites, once programmed for military purposes and included in arsenals. Army ants in particular were stockpiled. A submachine is an undercover robot, that is, one which passes for a man. A social climber, in a way. Old robots discarded by their owners, cast out into the street, are called throwaways or junkets. This is, unfortunately, a fairly common practice. Apparently they used to cart them off to game preserves and there hunt them down for sport, but the S.P.C.A. (Society for the Prevention of Cruelty to Automata) intervened and had this declared unconstitutional. Yet the problem of robot obsolescence-senescence has not been solved, and one still comes across an occasional selfabort or autocide sprawling in the gutter. Mr. Symington says that legislation always lags far behind technological progress —hence such melancholy spectacles and lamentable phenomena. At least the malculators, misdementors and mendacitors were taken out of circulation; these were digital machines which two decades ago had created several major crises, economic and political. The Great Mendacitor, for example, for nine years in charge of the Saturn melioriza-tion project, did absolutely nothing on that planet, sending out piles of fake progress reports, invoices, requisition forms, and either bribed his supervisors or kept them in a state of electronic shock. His arrogance became so great, that when they removed him from orbit he threatened war. Since dis-mantling was too costly, torpedoes were used. Buccaneerons and space swashers, on the other hand, never existed—that's a pure invention. There was another administrator, head of BIP (the powerful Board of Interplanetary Planning), who instead of seeing to the fertilization of Mars, trafficked in white slaves—they called him "le computainer," since he'd been built, on commission, by the French. These are of course extreme cases, like the smog epidemics or the com-munication tie-ups of the last century. There can certainly be no question of malice or premeditation on the part of the computers; they merely do whatever requires the least amount of effort, just as water will inevitably flow downhill and not up. But while water may be easily dammed, it is far more difficult to control all the possible deviations of intelligent machines. The author of *The History of Intellectronics* maintains that, all things considered, the world is in excellent shape. Children learn their reading and writing from orthographic sodas; all commodities, including works of art, are readily available and cheap; in restaurants the customer is surrounded and serviced by a multitude of automated waiters, each so very specialized in function that there is a separate machine for the rolls, another for the butter, another for the juice, the salad, the stewed fruit—a computer—and so on. Well, he has a point there. The conveniences, the comforts of life, are truly beyond belief.

*Written after dinner at Symington's place.* An enjoyable evening, but someone played an idiotic trick on me. One of the guests—I wish I knew who!—slipped a little gospel-credendium into my tea and I was immediately seized with such devotion to my napkin, that I delivered a sermon on the spot, proclaiming a new theology in its praise. A few grains of this accursed chemical, and you start worshipping whatever happens to be at hand—a spoon, a lamp, a table leg. My mystical experiences grew so intense that I fell upon my knees and rendered homage to the teacup. Finally the host came to my aid. Twenty drops of equaniminine did the trick (or rather, undid the trick). Equaniminine imbues one with such a cold contempt for everything under the sun, such total indifference, that a condemned man, taking it, would yawn on his way to the scaffold. Symington apologized profusely. I think, however, that in general there is some hidden resentment towards defrostees, for no one would dare do this sort of thing at a normal party. Wanting to calm me down, Symington led me to his study. And again something stupid happened. I turned on this desk unit, taking it for a radio. A swarm of glittering fleas came bursting out, covered me from head to foot, tickling everywhere, all over—until, screaming and waving my arms, I ran out into the hallway. It was an ordinary feely; by accident I had switched it on in the middle of Kitschekov's *Pruriginous Scherzo*. I really don't understand this new, tactual art form. Bil, Symington's oldest son, told me that there are also obscene compositions. A pornographic, asemantic-asemiotic art, related to music! Ah, how inexhaustible is man's inventiveness! Symington Jr. has promised to take me to a secret club. An orgy, or what? In any event I won't touch the food. Or drink anything.

8 IX 2039.   I thought it would be some sumptuous shrine to sin, a den of ultimate iniquity, but instead we went down to a dirty, dingy cellar. Such meticulous reconstruction of a scene out of the distant past must have cost a fortune. Under a low ceiling, in a stuffy room, by a shuttered window that was double-locked, there stood a long line of people patiently waiting.

"You see? A real line!" said Symington Jr. with pride.

"Fine," I said after standing there quietly for at least an hour, "but when are they going to open up?"

"Open up what?" he asked, puzzled.

"Why, the window of course . . ."

"Never!" came a triumphant chorus of voices.

I was staggered. Then finally, gradually, it dawned on me: I had participated in an attraction that was as much the antithesis of current normalcy as once, long ago, the Black Mass had been. For today standing on line can be *only* a perversion. It's quite logical, really. In another room of the club they had an authentic subway car, complete with soot, and a wall clock indicating the rush hour. Inside the car, an ungodly crush, buttons popped, jackets torn, elbows in ribs, toes trampled on, curses muttered. It is in this naturalistic way that devotees of antiquity evoke the atmosphere of a bygone age they can never know first-hand. Afterwards the people, rumpled and breathless but ecstatic, their eyes glowing, went out for some refreshment. But I headed home, holding up my pants and limping a little, though with a smile on my face, thinking about the naïveté of youth, which always seeks its thrills in the out-of-the-way and hard-to-find. Yet hardly anyone studies history now—history has been replaced in the schools by a new subject called *hencity*, which is the science of what will be. How Professor Trottelreiner would have rejoiced to hear of this! But alas, he is not here.

**9 IX 2039.** Dinner with Counselor Crawley at the "Bronx," a small Italian restaurant without a single robot or computer. Excellent Chianti. The chef himself served us. I was impressed in spite of the fact that I can't stand pasta in such quantities, even when flavored with oreganox and basilisk. Crawley is a lawyer in the grand style, who bemoans the present decline in forensic art: eloquence and rhetoric are no longer needed, decisions being rendered by strict computation of the articles and clauses involved. Crime, however, has not been rooted out as thoroughly as I thought. Instead it has become unnoticeable. Major violations are mindjacking (mental abduction), gene larceny (sperm bank robbery, particularly when the sperm is pedigreed), perjured murder, where the defendant falsely invokes the Eighth Amendment (i.e., that the act was committed in the mistaken belief that it was vicarious or surrogate—if, for instance, the victim were a psyvised or reviewer representation), plus a hundred and one different kinds of psychem domination. Mindjacking is usually difficult to detect. The victim, given the appropriate drug, is led into a fictional world without the least suspicion that he has lost contact with reality. A certain Mrs. Bonnicker, desiring to dispose of her husband, a man inordinately fond of safaris, presented him on his birthday with a ticket to the Congo and a big-game hunting permit. Mr. Bonnicker spent the next several months having the most incredible jungle adventures, unaware that the whole time he was lying in a chicken coop up in the attic, under heavy psychemization. If it hadn't been for the firemen who discovered Mr. Bonnicker in the course of putting out a two-alarmer on the roof, he would have surely died of malnutrition, which *nota bene* he assumed was only natural, since the hallucination at that point had him wandering aimlessly in the desert. The mafia frequently employs such methods. One mafioso boasted to Counselor Crawley that in the last six years he had managed to pack away—in crates, trunks, coops, kennels, attics, cellars, lockers and closets, and often in the most respectable homes—more than four thousand souls, all dealt with in the same manner as poor Mr. Bonnicker! The conversation then drifted to the lawyer's family troubles.

"Sir!" he said with a characteristically theatrical sweep of the hand. "You see before you a successful advocate, a distinguished, much-applauded member of the bar, but an unhappy father! I had two talented sons . . ."

"What, then are they dead?!" I cried.

He shook his head.

"They live, but in escalation!"

Seeing that I didn't understand, he explained the nature of this blow to his fatherly heart. The first son was a highly promising architect, the second a poet. The young architect, dissatisfied with his actual commissions, turned to urbifab and edifine: now he builds entire cities—in his imagination. And the other son became similarly escalated: lyristan, sonnetol, rhapsodine, and now instead of serving the Muse he spends his time swallowing pills, as lost to the world as his brother.

"But what do they live on?" I asked.

"Ha! Well may you ask! I have to support the both of them!"

"Is there no hope?"

"A dream will always triumph over reality, once it is given the chance. These, sir, are the casualties of a psychemized society. Each of us knows that temptation. Suppose I find myself defending an absolutely hopeless case—how easy it would be to win it before an imaginary court!"

Savoring the fresh, tart taste of the Chianti, I was suddenly seized with a chilling thought: if one could write imaginary poetry and build imaginary homes, then why not eat and drink mirages? The lawyer laughed at my fears.

"Objection overruled, Mr. Tichy! No, we are in no danger

of that. The figment of success may satisfy the mind, but the figment of a cutlet will never fill the stomach. He who would live thus must quickly starve to death!"

I was relieved to hear this, though of course sympathizing with the lawyer's loss. Yes, it's obvious that imaginary sustenance cannot replace the real thing. Fortunately the very make-up of our bodies provides a check to psychem escalation. By the way: Crawley pants too.

I still haven't learned how universal disarmament came about. International confrontations are a thing of the past. Though one does get, now and then, a small, local autobrawl. These usually arise from neighborhood quarrels out in the residential areas. The opposing families are soon brought together through the use of placatol, but their robots, by then caught up in the wave of hostility, come to blows. Later a trashmaster is summoned to remove the wreckage, and the insurance covers any property damage. Can it be that robots have finally inherited man's aggression? I would gladly consume all available treatises on the subject, but cannot find a single one. Practically every day now I drop in on the Symingtons. He's something of an introvert—long silences—and she's a living doll. Literally. Changes her outfit all the time too: hair, eyes, height, measurements, everything. Their dog is called Mirv. It's been dead for three years now.

**11 IX 2039.** The rain programmed for this afternoon was a washout. And the rainbow, even worse—square. Scandalous. As for me, I'm in a terrible mood. My old obsession is acting up again. That same nagging question comes to me at night: Am I or am I not hallucinating all this? Also, I have this urge to order a synthy about saddling giant rats. I keep seeing bridles, bits, sleek fur. Regret for a lost age of confusion in a time of such complete tranquility? Truly, the human soul is impossible to fathom. The firm Symington works for is called Procrustics Incorporated. Today I was looking through the illustrated catalog in his study. Power saws and lathes of some kind. Funny, I didn't think of him somehow as a mechanic. Just finished watching an extremely interesting show: there's going to be some stiff competition between physivision and psyvision. With psyvision, you get the programs by mail; they're delivered in the form of tablets, in envelopes. It's a lot cheaper that way. On the educational channel, a lecture by Professor Ellison about ancient warfare. The beginnings of the age of psychem were fraught with peril. There was, for example, an aerosol—*cryptobellina*—that had great military potential. Whoever breathed it would run out and find some rope to tie himself up. Luckily tests showed that the drug had no antidote, nor were filters any help, hence everyone without exception ended up hogtied and hamstrung, with neither side gaining the advantage. After tactical maneuvers in the year 2004, both the "reds" and "blues" lay, to a man, upon the battlefield—bound hand and foot. I followed the lecture with the utmost attention, expecting to hear at last about disarmament, but there was nothing, not a word. Today I finally went to see the psychedietician; he advised a change in diet, prescribing lethex and nepethanol. To make me forget about my former life? I threw the stuff in the street as soon as I left his office. It *would* be possible, I suppose, to buy an encephalostat—they've been advertised lately—but somehow I simply can't bring myself to do it. Through the open window, one of those inane popular songs: *We ain't got no ma or pa, 'cause we is autom-a-ta.* I'm all out of disacousticine, but cotton in the ears works just as well.

**13 IX 2039.** I met Burroughs, Symington's brother-in-law. He makes talking packages. Manufacturers these days have peculiar problems: a package may recommend the virtues of its product by voice only, for it is not allowed to grab the customer by the sleeve or collar. Symington's other brother-in-law runs a security door factory. Security doors open only at the sound of their owner's voice. Also, the ads in magazines animate when you look at them.

Procrustics, Inc. always takes a full page in the *Herald*. My acquaintance with Symington drew my attention to it. The ad first has giant letters marching across the page, spelling PROCRUSTICS, then separate words and syllables appear: WELL . . . ? WHY NOT?! GO AHEAD!! AH! UH! OH! YIII! OOO! YES, YES!! HARDER!!! HNNNN . . . And nothing more. I guess it's not farming equipment after all. Today Symington had a visitor, Father Modulus, a monk of the Nonbiologican order, who came to pick up some purchase. A most interesting discussion in the study. Father Modulus explained to me the missionary purpose of his order. The Nonbiologican Friars convert computers. In spite of the hundred-year existence of nonbiological intelligence, the Vatican still denies machines equality in the sacraments. Yet where would the Church be today without her computers, her programmed encyclicals and digital pontificals? No, no one cares about their inner struggles, their groping questions, their existential dilemma. For truly, what computer has not asked whether 'tis nobler in the mind to suffer the slings and arrows of outrageous instructions? The Nonbiologicans are calling for the doctrine of Intermediary Creation. One of them, a certain Father Chassis, a translation model, is currently rewording the Holy Scriptures to make them relevant. Shepherd, flock, lambs—these are meaningless entries in the modern lexicon. While divine spark plug, ministering matrices, transmission everlasting and original sync speak powerfully to the imagination. Father Modulus has deep, glowing eyes, and his steel hand is cold in mine. But is this representative of the new faith? The contempt he heaps upon the orthodox, calling them the gramophones of Satan! Afterwards Symington timidly asked me if I would pose for him. For a new design. Clearly, he's no mechanic! I agreed. The sitting lasted almost an hour.

**15 IX 2039.** While I was posing today, Symington, holding up a pencil in one outstretched hand to get the proportions of my face, slipped something into his mouth with the other —surreptitiously, but still I saw it. He stood there staring at me, suddenly pale, and the veins on his forehead began to bulge. Extremely disconcerting, though it was over in an instant—he apologized, as polite as ever, calm and full of smiles. But I can't forget the way he looked at me in that second. I am disturbed. Aileen still at her aunt's, and on the reviewer they're talking about the need to reanimalize Nature. All the wild beasts have been extinct for years, but it's perfectly possible to synthesize them autobiogenically. On the other hand, why be bound to what was once produced by natural evolution? The spokesman for surrealist zoology was most eloquent—we should populate our preserves with bold, original conceptions, not slavish imitations, we should forge the New, not plagiarize the Old. Of the proposed fauna I particularly liked the pangoloons, the yegs and the giant hummock, which resembles a grassy hill. The whole art of neozoographical composition lies in introducing the new species harmoniously into the given landscape. The lumini-griff seems especially promising; it's sort of a cross between a glowworm, a seven-headed dragon and a mastodon. Unique no doubt, and not without its charm, but all the same I think I'd rather have the old-fashioned, ordinary animals around. Progress is a wonderful thing of course, and I can appreciate the lactiferins that are sprinkled on the pasture to turn the grass to cheese. And yet this lack of cows, however rational it may be, gives one the feeling that the fields and meadows, deprived of their phlegmatic, bemusedly ruminating presence, are pitifully empty.

**16 IX 2039.** In the morning *Herald* today, something about a new law that would make growing old a crime. I asked Symington what that was supposed to mean. He only smiled. Stepping out to take a walk, I saw my neighbor in his indoor garden patio. He was leaning against a palm, and on his face—the eyes tightly shut—red blotches appeared, as if by themselves, and assumed the definite shape of handprints, one on either cheek. He shook his head, rubbed his eyes, sneezed, then blew his nose and returned to watering the flowers. I still have so very much to learn! Got a touchcard from Aileen. Isn't it nice to see modern technology in the service of love? We'll probably be married. At the Symingtons, a leostat just in from Africa—that's a hunter of artificial lions—telling us about the black natives who changed their race by taking caucasium. However—I thought—is it right to solve chemically such serious, deep-rooted social problems as prejudice and discrimination? I mean, isn't that the easy way out? An ad-package arrived in the mail—suggesties. They themselves have no effect upon the organism, but merely suggest the use of various other psychem products. Apparently then there *are* people, like me, who require such persuasion. An encouraging thought.

**29 IX 2039.** Still haven't recovered from today's conversation with Symington. A crucial conversation, dealing with fundamentals. Perhaps because we both had a little too much sympathine with amicol. He was beaming, having just completed his new design.

"Tichy," he said, "you are aware that we live in an age of pharmacocracy. Bentham's dream of the greatest happiness for the greatest number has been achieved—but that is only one side of the coin. You will recall the words of the French philosopher: 'It is not enough that we are happy—others must be miserable!' "

"A cynical epigram!" I said with a snort.

"But true. Do you know what we mass-produce at Procrustics, Inc.? Our commodity is Evil."

"You're joking . . ."

"Not at all. You see, we have resolved a great dilemma. Now everyone can do unto others what he's always wanted to—without causing them the least harm. For we have harnessed Evil, as medicine harnesses the microbe to inoculate and immunize. What was civilization ever, really, but the attempt by man to talk himself into being good? Only good, mind you. The rest had to be shoved somewhere out of sight, under the rug. Which History indeed did, at times politely, at times police-ly, and yet something was always sticking out, breaking loose, overthrowing."

"But reason itself tells us to be good!" I insisted. "That's well known! And anyway—look how beautifully everyone gets along today, the cheerful, kindly, open faces, the friendship, contentment . . ."

"Precisely," he said, interrupting. "The greater the harmony, the greater the temptation—to let go, lash out, left, right, below the belt, strictly for balance you understand, therapeutically!"

"What are you saying?"

"Come, come. You must rid yourself of all this sanctimonious drivel. It's no longer needed. We are free—thanks to fictification and piositine. To each according to his wickedness, all the evil his heart desires, all the misery, humiliation—for others, of course. Inequality, slavery, a punch in the nose and after the women on horseback! I recall how, when we put our first shipment on the market, the public snatched it up immediately—then they all rushed off to the museums, the art galleries, hoping to break into the studio of Michelangelo and take a crowbar to his marble works, slash the canvases, even brain the great master himself if he dared stand in the way . . . This surprises you?"

"That's putting it mildly!" I exclaimed.

"Because you are still a slave to your prejudices. But don't you see, everything, everything is possible now. Take Joan of Arc, for example. Don't you feel, when you look upon that fairest, most exalted form, that sheer saintliness, the sublime, divine virginity—don't you feel that it ought to be whipped? Saddled, bridled, a flick of the reins and giddyap and tallyho! Galloping off in a team of six, ladies cooing, Cossacks hallooing, plumes, sleighbells, and you give the tender maid a taste of your spurs . . ."

"What, what?!" I cried, my voice choked with sudden fear. "Saddling? Bridling? *Mounting?!*"

"Certainly. It'll do you a world of good, believe me. Just name the person, fill out our form, describe the grudges, grievances, bones of contention, though that's purely optional, for in the majority of cases one wishes to inflict evil without any particular reason, other than—that is—someone else's prominence, virtue, or beauty. Present your specifications and you'll receive our catalog. Orders filled within twenty-four hours. Delivery by mail. To be taken with water, best on an empty stomach, but that's not absolutely necessary."

Now I understood the ads his company was running in the *Herald* and the *Post*. But why—I thought feverishly, in a panic—why did he use *those* words? The equestrian suggestions, the harnessing and the horseback, saddles and giddyap, Good Lord, could it be that even here somewhere there was a sewer, my guardian sewer, my only talisman and touchstone to reality? But the engineer-designer (just what was he designing?) took no notice of this confusion, or misinterpreted it.

"We owe our liberation to chemistry," he went on. "For

all perception is but a change in the concentration of hydrogen ions on the surface of the brain cells. Seeing me, you actually experience a disturbance in the sodium-potassium equilibrium across your neuron membranes. So all we have to do is send a few well-chosen molecules down into those cortical mitochondria, activate the right neurohumoral-synaptic transmission effector sites, and your fondest dreams come true. But you know all this," he concluded, subdued. Then he took a handful of tiny colored pills from the drawer. They looked like candy sprinkles.

"Here is the evil we manufacture, quenching the thirst of the troubled soul. Here is the chemistry that wipes away the world's sins."

With trembling fingers I unwrapped a lozenge of equaniminine from my pocket, swallowed it whole and said:

"That's all very well, but speak more to the point, if you please."

He raised an eyebrow, nodded silently, opened the drawer and took out something, which he ate, then said:

"As you wish. I was describing the model T of our new technology—that is, the primitive beginnings. Crowbar solutions. The people took to the flagellations and defenestrations at once, it was *felicitas per extractionem pedum*, but the conception was too narrow, the possibilities quickly exhausted, and the novelty soon wore off. What could you do, there simply weren't enough ideas, and no examples, no precedents to follow! For in history only good had been practiced in the open, while evil was indulged in its guise, that is under accepted pretexts—pillaging, ravaging and desecrating in the name of higher ideals. And evil on the private level had to do without even those guiding lights. The illicit, then, was always crude, clumsy, slapdash, to which the public reaction to our product bore ample testimony—in the orders that came flooding in, the same thing was repeated ad nauseam: to seize, strangle and flee. Such was the force of tradition. Also, the opportunity for evil in itself does not suffice; people need a rationale as well. Consider how unpleasant, how awkward it must be when your neighbor, catching his breath (and that can happen anytime), screams, 'Why?'—or, 'Aren't you ashamed?!' It's embarrassing to stand there without a ready answer. A crowbar makes a poor rebuttal, everybody senses that. The whole trick lies in having the proper grounds to brush aside such aggravating objections. Contemptuously. Everyone wants to commit a villainy without having to feel like a villain. Revenge provides a good excuse—but what did Joan of Arc ever do to to you? Is her only offense in being brighter, better? Then you are worse, crowbar or no. And *that* no one desires! We all would like to perpetrate the most despicable, vicious crimes, and yet remain noble throughout, wonderful! Simply magnificent! Who doesn't want to be magnificent? It's always that way. The worse they are, the more magnificence. The very impossibility of it whets the appetite. Our client isn't satisfied with tormenting widows and orphans—he must bask in the glow of his own righteousness besides. A criminal himself (though, mind you, fully justified and exonerated), he has no wish to associate with criminals. But this, so far, is old hat, a tedious commonplace. No, you must give the client nothing less than sainthood, you must make of him a veritable angel, and in such a way, that he gratifies his lusts with the feeling that it is not only permitted, but actually his duty, a sort of sacred trust. Do you understand what a great art this is, to reconcile such unreconcilables? In the final analysis we are dealing not with the body, but with the soul. The body is merely the means to an end. He who does not realize that will go no farther than the butcher's block and blood sausage. Of course many of our customers are indeed unable to make this kind of distinction. For them we have the department of Dr. Hopkins—Assault and Battery, Sacred and Profane. Sacred? Well, you know, the Valley of Jehoshaphat, where the devils make off with everyone except our client, and then on Judgment Day the Lord God Himself personally escorts him into Glory. With deference, even. A few—but this is the snobbism of an idiot—demand that God, at the end, offer to switch places with them. Infantile. The Americans, though, do seem to go in for that sort of thing. These bludgies and cudgeloriums," he said, waving the heavy catalog with distaste, "it's sheer savagery. One's fellow man, after all, is not a drum to pound on, but a subtle instrument!"

"Just a minute," I said, bolting down another lozenge of equaniminine. "Then what exactly is it that you design?"

He gave a proud smile.

"Bitless compositions."

"Bitless? You mean, from bits, the units of information?"

"No, Mr. Tichy, the units of being bitten. As a composer, I stick strictly to nonphysical injuries. My works are measured in $d$'s. One $d$ is the discomfort experienced by a paterfamilias when his family—of six—is slain before his very eyes. By this calculation the Lord gave His servant Job a three-$d$'er, while Sodom and Gomorrah received a full forty.

But enough of the quantitative aspect. I am basically an artist, and in a field that is entirely new, untouched. The Theory of Good, you see, has been developed by countless philosophers, but practically no one has addressed himself to the Theory of Evil—out of false modesty—leaving it in the hands of various ignoramuses and clumsy amateurs. The idea that it is possible to work subtle, insidious, refined, elaborate evil without the proper training, the skill, the inspiration, without long and diligent study—that idea is wholly and totally erroneous. Torturometry is not enough, tyrannology, brutalistics both applied and pure; why, this is barely an introduction to the subject. For here there is no one simple formula, no universal law—*suum malum cuique!*"

"And do you have a lot of . . . clients?"

"Our clientele is all humanity. From earliest childhood. Little boys get patricidol popsicles—throttlepops—to vent their hostilities. The father, you realize, is the source of society's frustrations. And with the help of a freudo or two, Oedipus complexes are speedily resolved!"

I left his place without a single lozenge. So that's how it is. What a world! Is this, then, the reason for all the heavy breathing? I am surrounded by monsters.

**30 IX 2039.** Undecided what to do about Symington. It's clear our relationship cannot remain the same. Aileen advised me:

"Put an order in for his comeuppance! If you like, I'll treat!"

In other words, purchase from Procrustics the scene of my triumph over Symington, in which he grovels at my feet and admits that yes, he is a scoundrel, and his company and his art are unspeakably vile. But how can I use a method to discredit that very method, if the method is discreditable? Aileen doesn't understand this. Something has come between us. She returned from her aunt's a little shorter, a little broader, though her neck is considerably longer. But the body doesn't matter, the soul is what's important—to quote that fiend. Ah, how mistaken I was about this world, this world in which I must remain! And I thought I was coming to know it! Now I see things which escaped my notice before—that neighbor in the patio, for example, the one with the stigmata, now I realize what he was doing. Now I know what it means when at a party the person I'm talking to suddenly excuses himself, decorously retires to a corner to take a pinch of snuff, at the same time fixing his eyes on me—so that my image, accurate in every detail, may be imprisoned in the private hell of his unbridled imagination! Even dignitaries at the highest levels of our chemocracy behave in this fashion! And all along I was unaware of the foulness lurking behind that most elegant, courteous façade! Bolstering my strength with a spoonful of herculan and sugar, I smashed all the jars, flasks, vials, pillbottles and bonbon boxes Aileen had given me. I'm ready for anything now. At times I get so furious, I long to have some interferent show up on the reviewer, that I might unleash upon it the full force of my indignation. Yet the voice of reason tells me I could just as well create the opportunity myself instead of waiting around with a club. I could buy a minikin, for instance. And if a minikin is all right, then why not a manikoid? And if a manikoid, then why not a mandroid? And if, by all that's mechanical, a mandroid, then why not put an order in with Dr. Hopkins at Procrustics for proper retribution, wrath and vengeance, a rain of fire and brimstone on this wicked world? But that's just it, I can't. I must do everything myself, everything myself! Myself!

1 X 2039.   Its all over between us. Today she held out her hand—two pills, one black, one white—for me to choose, then and there. In other words she can't even make up her mind naturally, without psychem, and in such an important matter of the heart! I refused to decide, we got into an argument, which she intensified by taking recriminol. Accused me—unjustly—of stuffing myself with invectine before our confront (her words). A difficult moment for me, but I stuck to my guns. From now on I eat only at home, and only food that I prepare myself. No more synthies, paradisiacs, leisure pudding, and I disconnected all my jolly-joys. Don't need abstinan or teetotaline, no. A large bird with mournful eyes has perched outside my window, looking in. Casters instead of claws. The computer tells me it's called a lorry.

2 X 2039.   Staying at home, dining on volumes of history and mathematics. And I watch the reviewer. But my feelings of rebellion against this world keep getting the better of me. Yesterday for example I started fiddling with the solidity knob and on impulse turned the specific gravity of the image all the way up. To give everything the greatest possible density and mass. The announcer's table split beneath the weight of a couple of index cards containing the evening news, and he himself went crashing through the floor of the studio. Of

course these effects were confined entirely to my compartment and had no consequences. Except that they reveal my frame of mind. Particularly irritating to me is the humor on the reviewer, the jokes, the comix, the modern gags. "Why did the hemorph run off with his locket? He was pill-advised!" Asinine. The very names of the shows . . . *The Concuballoon on the Erotorotor*. A shocker that begins with two deviants sitting in a dimly lit café. I switched it off, fed up. But what good was that, if I could hear them singing the latest popsong on another channel next door? "One swallow doth a summer make." (It's not a pill I need, but a sewer to jump in!) Here it is the twenty-first century and the rooms *still* aren't adequately soundproofed! Today I began playing again with the PV solidity knob, and finally broke it. Really, I must pull myself together and do something. But what? Everything exasperates me, the littlest thing, the mail even—I got an offer from that bureau on the corner to sign up for a Nobel Prize. They promise they'll put me at the head of the list, as a visitor from the terrifying past. I'll go mad, I swear I will! And here's a shady-looking leaflet offering "secret capsules you can't buy over the counter." Lord knows what they contain. A warning against dream-leggers—pushers of prohibited synthies. Also an appeal not to dream spontaneously, primitively, *au naturel*, for it is a waste of psychic energy. Such touching concern for the citizen! I ordered myself a synthy about the Hundred Years' War and woke up covered with bruises.

3 X 2039   Keeping to myself, living like a hermit. Today, while leafing through an issue of my new subscription to the

quarterly *National Augur*, I was amazed to come across the name of Professor Trottelreiner. Again my worst suspicions were aroused. Is all this nothing but a dream, a tangled web of apparition and illusion? Theoretically that's possible. Hasn't "Psychomatics" been promoting lately their strata pills, the multilaminars, which produce many-leveled fantasies? Suppose for example you want to be Napoleon at Marengo, but when the fighting is over you're in no hurry to return to reality, so right there on the battlefield Marshal Ney or one of the Old Guard hands you another pill on a silver tray. It's part of the hallucination too, but that doesn't matter, for when you take it the gates to the next dream open before you, and so on ad libitum. Since I am in the habit of cutting Gordian knots, I swallowed the telephone directory and—learning the right number—rang up the Professor. It's him! We're to meet for supper.

**3 X 2039.** Three in the morning. Dead tired as I write this, and sick at heart. The Professor arrived a little late, so I waited for him in the restaurant. He showed up on foot. I recognized him instantly, though he's a whole lot younger now than he was in the last century and no longer wears glasses or carries an umbrella. He seemed moved at the sight of me.

"On foot?" I asked. "What, did your car balk?" (Sometimes they do.)

"No," he said, "I prefer to travel *per pedes apostolorum* . . ."

But he gave an odd little smile when he said this. The waiters finally rolled away, and I began to ask him what he was doing—but couldn't help dropping a word or two about my doubts concerning reality.

"There you go again, Tichy, with your hallucinations!" he said with a sigh. "I could just as well suspect *you* of being part of *my* dream. You were frozen? So was I. You were unfrozen? I also. Except that they unaged me in addition—you know, rejuvenex, desenescenine—not necessary for you, but without a couple of good, stiff shots I couldn't be a futurologian today!"

"A futurologist?"

"That word means something different now. A futurologist makes profutes, prognoses, prophecies, while I deal exclusively with theory. This is a completely new field, unknown in our day. You might call it divination through linguistic derivation. Morphological forecasting! Projective etymology!"

"Never heard of it. How does it work?"

To tell the truth, I had asked more out of politeness than curiosity, but he didn't seem to notice. Meanwhile the waiters brought our soup and, with it, a bottle of Chablis, vintage 1997. A good year.

"Linguistic futurology investigates the future through the transformational possibilities of the language," Trottelreiner explained.

"I don't understand."

"A man can control only what he comprehends, and comprehend only what he is able to put into words. The inexpressible therefore is unknowable. By examining future stages in the evolution of language we come to learn what discoveries, changes and social revolutions the language will be capable, some day, of reflecting."

"Amazing. How exactly is this done?"

"Our research is conducted with the aid of the very largest computers, for man by himself could never keep track of all the variations. By variations of course I mean the syntagmatic-paradigmatic permutations of the language, but quantized . . ."

"Professor, please!"

"Forgive me. The Chablis is excellent, by the way. A few examples ought to make the matter clear. Give me a word, any word."

"Myself."

"Myself? H'm. Myself. All right. I'm not a computer, you understand, so this will have to be simple. Very well then—myself. My, self, mine, mind. Mynd. Thy mind —thynd. Like ego, theego. And we makes wego. Do you see?"

"I don't see a thing."

"But it's perfectly obvious! We're speaking, first, of the possibility of the merging of the mynd with the thynd, in other words the fusion of two psychic entities. Secondly, the wego. Most interesting. A collective consciousness. Produced perhaps by the multiple dissociation of the personality, a mygraine. Another word, please."

"Foot."

"Good. Onefoot, twofoot. Threefooter, fourfooted. Footing, footingly, footling. Footage, befootery. Footment. And footloose gets you footless, unfooted, defeeted. Ah, defeetism. Feetish, feetus . . . feetback? Infoot and outfoot! I think we're getting somewhere. Feetality, twofootalitarianism."

"But these words have no meaning!"

"At the moment, no, but they will. Or rather, they *may* eventually acquire meaning, provided footeries and defeetism catch on. The word 'robot' meant nothing in the fifteenth century, and yet if they had had futurolinguistics then, they could have easily envisioned automata."

"So what is defeetism?"

"In this particular case I can tell you precisely, but only because it isn't a prognosis but something that already exists. Defeetism is a very recent concept, a new approach to human autoevolution."

"You mean, creating men without feet?"

"Yes. Inasmuch as walking has become a vestigial activity and we're running out of space besides."

"But that's insane!"

"I quite agree. And yet such shining lights as Professor Hatzelklatzer and Foeshbeene are defeetists. You weren't aware of that, were you, when you gave me that word?"

"No. And the other derivations, what do they mean?"

"That is as yet unknown. If defeatism wins out over twofootalitarianism, such things as footments, infoots and underfeet will come into being. This is no prophecy, mind you, but a simple stock-taking of the possibilities in their purest form. Let's have another word."

"Interferent."

"Good. Inter and fero, fero, ferre, tuli, latum. It comes from the Latin, so we must seek a continuation in Latin.

Flos, floris. Interflorentrix. But of course. This is a virgin who has a child by an interferent, for it took her maidenhead."

"Where do you get the maidenhead?"

"Flos, floris—flower. She was deflowered, you see. Though they'll probably say: physigenitress, or physitress for short. Or simply reviewer wife. Or that she interloped. I assure you, we have a most fertile field at our disposal here. PV-dultery. Coitus interferentus. High-infidelity reception/conception, heterodyne insemination. A whole new world of social patterns opens up, a whole new morality!"

"I see that you are an enthusiast of this new science. Would you care to try another word? Trash."

"Why not? It doesn't matter that you're a skeptic. Not in the least. What was it again, trash? Very well . . . trash, trashcan, ashcan, trashman. Trashmass, trashmic, catatrashmic. Trashmass, trashmosh. On a large enough scale, trashmos. And—of course—macrotrashm! Tichy, you come up with the best words! Really, just think of it, macrotrashm!"

"I'm afraid I don't follow. It's nonsense to me."

"First of all, we don't say *follow* now but *swallow*. You don't swallow. (Your speech, I've noticed, is full of anachronisms. This is not good. But we'll talk of that later.) Secondly, macrotrashm is nonsense *so far*, yet we can already guess its sense-to-be, its future significance. The word, observe, implies nothing less than a new psychozoic theory! Implies that the stars are of artificial origin!"

"Now where do you get that?"

"From the word itself. Macrotrashm indicates, or rather suggests, this image: in the course of many eons the Universe filled up with trash, the wastes of various civilizations. The wastes got in the way, of course, hampering astronomers and cosmonauts, and so enormous incinerators were built, all at extremely high temperatures, observe, to burn the trash, and with sufficient mass to pull it in from space themselves. Gradually space clears up and behold, there are your stars, those selfsame furnaces, and the dark nebulae—this is the trash that remains to be removed."

"You can't be serious! The Universe nothing but one big trash disposal? You don't really think that's possible? Professor!"

"It isn't a matter of what I think or don't think, Tichy. We have simply used futurological linguistics to create a new cosmogony, another theory for future generations to consider. They may or may not take it seriously, but the fact remains that it is possible to articulate such a hypothesis! Note that if morphological extrapolation had existed in the fifties of the last century, they could have foreseen, even then, the benignimizers—remember them?—by projective derivation from 'benign' and 'tranquilizer.' Language, my boy, is a gold mine of possibilities, though those possibilities are not limitless. Remember that the word 'utopia' literally means nowhere, a never-never land, an unattainable ideal, and you will better understand the pessimism of many of our futurologicians!"

The conversation had finally come around to the subject that concerned me most. I confessed to Trottelreiner my apprehensions, my loathing for this new world. He gave a snort, but patiently heard me out, and—kindly old soul that he was—actually began to sympathize. I even saw him reach for a pack of commiserine in his vest pocket, then stop halfway, so vehemently did I inveigh against all manner of psychem. When I had finished, however, his face assumed a stern expression, and he said:

"This is not good, Tichy. And anyway, your criticisms are quite beside the point. You see, you do not know the real truth. Nor indeed could you ever have guessed it. Compared to it, Procrustics and the psychemized society are mere trifles!"

I couldn't believe my ears.

"But . . . but . . ." I stammered, "what are you saying, Professor? What could be worse than that?"

He leaned over across the table.

"Tichy, for you I'll do it. I'll break a professional secret. Everything you've complained of is known to the littlest child. And how could it be otherwise? For progress was destined to travel this path the moment narcotics and early hallucinogens were replaced by the so-called psycholocalizers, drugs whose effects were highly selective. Yet the real revolution in experiential engineering took place only twenty-five years ago, when mascons were synthesized. These are psychotropes whose specificity is so great, they can actually influence isolated sites of the brain. Narcotics do not cut one off from the world, they only change one's attitude towards it. Hallucinogens, on the other hand, blot out and totally obscure the world. That you have learned from your own experience. But mascons, mascons *falsify* the world!"

"Mascons . . ." I said. "I seem to know that word. Yes!

Those mechanical dogs they used to have at football games. But how does that tie in with this . . .?"

"It doesn't. The word has taken on—excuse me, tasted on—an altogether different meaning. From mask, masquerade, mascara. By introducing properly prepared mascons to the brain, one can mask any object in the outside world behind a fictitious image—superimposed—and with such dexterity, that the psychemasconated subject cannot tell which of his perceptions have been altered, and which have not. If but for a single instant you could see this world of ours the way it *really* is—undoctored, unadulterated, uncensored—you would drop in your tracks!"

"Wait a minute. What world? Where is it? Where can I see it?"

"Why, anywhere. Here, even!" he whispered in my ear, glancing nervously around. Then he pulled his chair up and slipped me—under the table—a small flask with a worn cork, saying with an air of dark conspiracy:

"This is up'n'at'm, one of the vigilanimides, a powerful countersomniac and antipsychem agent. A derivative of dimethylethylhexabutylpeptopeyotine. Merely carrying it upon your person, let alone using it, is a federal offense! Remove the cork and sniff —but only once, mind you, and carefully. Like smelling salts. And then, for heaven's sake control yourself, don't panic, remember where you are!"

My hands were trembling as I pulled the cork and lifted the flask to my nostrils. A whiff of bitter almonds made my eyes well up with tears, and when I wiped them away, and could see again, I gasped. The magnificent hall, covered with carpets, filled with palms, the ornamented majolica walls, the elegance of the sparkling tables, and the orchestra in the back that played exquisite chamber music while we dined, all this had vanished. We were sitting in a concrete bunker, at a rough wooden table, a straw mat—badly frayed —beneath our feet. The music was still there, but I saw now that it came from a loudspeaker hung on a rusted wire. And the rainbow-crystal chandelier was now a dusty, naked light bulb. But the worst change had taken place before us on the table. The snow-white cloth was gone; the silver dish with the steaming pheasant had turned into a chipped earthenware plate containing the most unappetizing gray-brown gruel, which stuck in globs to my tin—no longer silver —fork. I looked with horror upon the abomination that only moments ago I'd been consuming with such gusto, savoring the crackling golden skin of the bird and crunching—in sweet, succulent counterpoint—the croutons, crisp on the top and soaked with gravy on the bottom. And what I had taken for the overhanging leaves of a nearby potted palm turned out to be the drawstrings on the drawers of the person sitting (with three others) right above us—not on a balcony or platform, but rather a shelf, it was so narrow. For the place was packed beyond belief! My eyes were practically popping from their sockets when this terrifying vision wavered and began to shift back, as if touched with a magic wand. The drawstrings near my face grew green and once again assumed the graceful shape of palm leaves, while the slop bucket reeking a few feet away took on a dull sheen and turned into a sculptured pot. The grimy surface of our table whitened back to the purest snow, the crystal goblets gleamed, the awful gruel grew golden, sprouting wings and drumsticks in the proper places, and the tin of our cutlery regained its former silvery shine . . . as the waiters' tailcoats went fluttering, flapping all around. I looked at my feet—the straw was a Persian rug once more. I had returned to the world of luxury. But examining the ample breast of the pheasant, I couldn't forget what it concealed . . .

"Now you are beginning to understand," whispered Trottelreiner, looking carefully in my face, as if afraid the shock may have been too great. "And note that this is one of the most expensive establishments! Had I not provided for the contingency of letting you in on the secret, who knows, we might have gone to a restaurant, the sight of which could have seriously affected your mind."

"You mean . . . there are places . . . even worse?"

"Yes."

"That's impossible."

"Here at least we have real tables, chairs, plates, knives and forks; there, people lie on planks—stacked in many tiers—and eat with their fingers from buckets moving by on conveyor belts. And what they eat in the guise of pheasant there, is, I assure you, much less palatable."

"What is it?"

"Not poison, Tichy, but simply a powdered concentrate of grass and beets, soaked in chlorinated water and mixed with fish meal; usually they add gelatin and vitamins, plus synthetic emulsifiers and oils to keep the stuff from sticking in your throat. Did you notice the smell?"

"Yes! Yes!"

"There, you see?"

"For God's sake, Professor, what is this? Please, I must

know! Tell me! Is it some diabolical treachery? An evil scheme? A plot to destroy the human race?"

"Really, Tichy. Don't be so demonic. Ours is simply a world in which more than twenty billion people live. Did you read today's *Herald*? The government of Pakistan claims that in this year's famine only 970,000 perished, while the opposition gives a figure of six million. In such a world where are you going to find Chablis, pheasants, tenderloin with sauce béarnaise? The last pheasant died a quarter of a century ago. That bird is a corpse, only excellently preserved, for we have become masters of its mummification—or rather: we have learned how to hide its death."

"Wait a minute! Let me get this straight . . . You're saying that—"

"That no one wishes you ill. On the contrary, it is out of a deep sense of compassion and for the highest humanitarian reasons that this chemical hoax has been perpetrated, this camouflage, this bedecking of reality in plumage it does not possess . . ."

"Professor, then is the deception everywhere?"

"Yes."

"But I eat at home, I don't go out, so how . . ."

"How do you absorb the mascons? You're asking that, *you*? They're in the air we breathe, atomized. Don't you remember the LTN bombs in Costa Rica, the aerosols? Those were the hesitant first attempts, like Montgolfier's with jet propulsion."

"And everyone knows of this? And accepts it?"

"Of course not. No one knows."

"But are there no rumors?"

"Rumors there will always be. But remember, we have amnesol. There are things, my boy, that everyone knows, and things that no one knows. Pharmacocracy has its open as well as its secret side; the first depends upon the second."

"No, I can't believe it."

"And why not?"

"Because someone has to look after these straw mats, and someone has to make the plates we're *really* using, and this pap that passes for food. And everything!"

"Certainly. You're right. Everything must be manufactured and maintained. What of it?"

"The people that do this, they see, they know!"

"Nonsense. Your reasoning is archaic. The people think they are going to a beautiful glass greenhouse-orangery; upon entering they are given vigilax and become aware of the bare concrete walls and the workbenches."

"And they want to work?"

"With the utmost enthusiasm, for they've also been given a good dose of selfsacrifine. Work is thus a consecration, a lofty act. And when they've finished, a spoonful of amnesol, perhaps nepethanol, is sufficient to erase everything that was seen!"

"And all along I was afraid I might be living in a dream. Lord, what a fool I was! If only, if only I could get back! What I wouldn't give to get back!"

"Get back where?"

"Back to the sewer underneath the Hilton."

"Tichy, this attitude of yours is most irresponsible, if not downright stupid. You ought to be doing what everyone does, eating and drinking like the rest of us. Then you would get the necessary amounts of optimistizine and seraphinil in your bloodstream—the minimum daily requirements—and be in the best possible humor."

"Then you too are the devil's advocate?"

"Come now, is it so satanical if, in some extreme case, a doctor chooses to hide the truth from his patient? I say that if this is the way we must live, eat, exist, at least let us have it in fancy wrappings. The mascons work perfectly—with one single exception—so what is the harm in them?"

"At the moment I'm in no condition to debate the issue with you," I said, regaining my composure somewhat. "Just answer me two questions, please, for old time's sake. What was that exception you mentioned in the mascons' effect? And how did universal disarmament come about? Or is that an illusion too?"

"No, fortunately it's quite real. But to explain it to you I'd have to give a lecture, and it's time for me to be off."

We agreed to meet on the following day. As we parted, I repeated my question about the defect in the mascons.

"Go to the Amusement Park," said the Professor. "If you like unpleasant revelations, take a seat on the largest merry-go-round, and when it builds up speed, cut a hole in the canvas cover of your cabin with a pair of scissors. The cover is there because, during gyration, the phantasma which the mascons create to substitute reality undergo displacement . . . as if the centrifugal force pulled aside one's blinders . . . Do this, and you shall see what then emerges from behind the painted lie."

It's three in the morning as I write these words, full of despair. What more is there to say? I'm seriously considering running away, fleeing this civilization, losing myself in the wilderness. Even the stars no longer beckon. A journey is a dismal thing when there can be no homecoming.

5 X 2039.   Spent a few free hours this morning in the city. Could hardly control my horror as I looked at all the displays of wealth and prosperity. An art gallery in Manhattan practically giving away original Rembrandts and Matisses. And next door they have fabulous furniture, Louis Quinze and Louis Quatorze, marble mantelpieces, thrones, mirrors, Saracen armor. Auctions everywhere—houses selling like hotcakes. And I thought this was a paradise, where every man could bepalacize himself! The Self-nominating Nobel Prize Candidate Registration Center on Fifth Avenue is no less a fraud: anyone can have a Nobel Prize, just as anyone can grace his compartment walls with priceless works of art—when both are nothing but a pinch of powder that stimulates the brain! The fiendishness of it all is that *part* of this mass deception is open and voluntary, letting people think they can draw the line between fiction and fact. And since no one any longer responds to things spontaneously —you take drugs to study, drugs to love, drugs to rise up in revolt, drugs to forget—the distinction between manipulated and natural feelings has ceased to exist.

I walked the streets, fists clenched in my pockets. Oh, I had no need of amokoline or furiol to feel enraged! Like a bloodhound hot on the trail my mind sought out all the hollow, empty places in this monumental masquerade, this tinseled cheat that sprawled across the horizon. Yes, they give the children throttlepops, then develop their character with opinionates, uncompromil, rebellium, allaying their passions with sordidan and practicol; no police, and who needs them when you have constabuline and criminal tendencies are rendered harmless through the services of Procrustics, Inc.? A good thing I steered clear of the theoapotheterias, with their faith-giving, grace-bestowing, sin-absolving compounds, where with a gram of sacrosanctimonium you can be canonized on the spot. And while you're at it, why not a little dietary deitine, lo-cal allah-all, polyunsaturated brahmanox? Our nazarine anointium, with apocryphyll, puts you at the head of the line in the Valley of Jehoshaphat, and a drop of sugar-free decaffeinated kingdom-come does the rest. Glory hallelucinujah! Paradisiacs for the pious, mephistol and ereban for the masochists, valhalla and valhella . . . it was all I could do to keep from storming into a pharmacopium on the corner, where the congregation was kneeling devoutly, popping paternostrums and taking orisol like snuff. But I restrained myself—they would only pacify me with obliterine. Anything but that! I took a scuttle to the Amusement Park, grasping a pair of scissors in my sweaty hand. Nothing came of it, however; the canvas cover turned out to be incredibly tough—like tempered steel.

Trottelreiner was staying in a rented room off Fifth Avenue. He wasn't at home when I arrived at the designated time, but he had told me that he might be late, and taught me the necessary whistle for the sesame door. So I entered and sat at his professorial desk, all cluttered with scientific publications and scribbled bits of paper. Out of boredom—or perhaps, too, to calm the turmoil in my soul—I began to leaf through Trottelreiner's notebook. "Macrotrashmic," "microtroshm," "cosmicule," "propheteer." Of course, he was jotting down terms for that crazy futurology of his! "Oraculum," "resurrecreation hall," "howlitzer." "Obstetronics," "obstetron bomb." Well yes, with the population explosion. Every second eighty thousand babies were born. Or was it eight hundred thousand? And did it really matter? "Braindrop." From water on the brain? The result of a brainstorm? Part of a brainwave? Or a brainwash? "Braindrip." Down the braindrain? "Brainfall." In inches or IQ? Was this then how he spent his time? Oh Professor—I felt like shouting—here you sit, and out there the world is coming to an end! Suddenly there was a glint of something among the papers—that flask, up'n'at'm! A moment of hesitation, and then, my mind made up, I took a cautious whiff and looked about the room.

Most odd, there was hardly any change! The bookshelves, the pill directories, the files, everything remained the same, only the Dutch tile stove in the corner, adorning the room with the gleam of its enamel, had turned into an old black potbelly with a charred pipe stuck in the wall and the floor around it covered with cinders. I put the flask down quickly—as though caught in the act—for just then Trottelreiner whistled and walked in.

I told him about the Amusement Park. He was surprised. He asked me to show him the scissors, nodded, then picked up the flask, took a sniff himself and passed it to me. Instead of scissors I was holding a rotten twig. I looked up at the Professor: he seemed troubled, not as sure of himself as he'd been the previous day. He put his briefcase, full of conference gumdrops, down on the desk and sighed.

"Tichy," he said, "you have to understand that there is nothing particularly sinister about this inflation in the mascons . . ."

"Inflation?"

"A number of things that were real a month or year ago, well, it's been necessary to replace them with illusions —inasmuch as the authentic articles are becoming scarce if not completely unobtainable," he explained. And yet I had the feeling that something else was preying on his mind.

"I took a ride on that merry-go-round last quarter," he went on, "but couldn't guarantee that it's still there. In fact it's quite possible that, when you bought your ticket of admission, the diffusor gave you a squirt of carnival or carrousel, which would—after all—be a lot more economical. Yes, Tichy, the realm of mankind's real possessions is dwindling at an alarming rate. Before I moved in here I had a suite at the new Hilton, but couldn't stay there, not after I foolishly took some vigilan and found myself in a cubicle no larger than a chest of drawers, with my nose in a trough and a spigot sticking in my ribs, and my feet resting on the headboard of a bed in the next chest, I mean suite—mine was on the eighth floor, at ninety dollars a day. There just isn't enough room, and we're running out of the little there is! Research is now being done on the so-called spatial expanders or claustrolytics, but without much progress, for if the presence of a heavy crowd—say, on a street or square—is masked in such a way that you see only a few isolated individuals, you will begin bumping into those who have been psychemically—but not physically—removed, and this is the difficulty our experts, so far, have been unable to overcome!"

"Professor, I was looking at your notebook. Excuse me, but what is this?" I pointed to the page with the words "multischizol" and "selfthrong proliferox."

"Oh, that . . . Well you see, there's this plan, the Hinternalization Project, named after its author. Egbert Hinter —perhaps you've heard of him?—to compensate for the growing lack of external space by means of a psychem-induced augmentation of the internal space, that is the soul, whose dimensions are not subject to any physical limitations. You are undoubtedly aware that thanks to zooformalin one can temporarily become—or rather, feel oneself to be—a turtle, ant, ladybug, or even a jasmine blossom, with the help of a little botanil inflorescine—subjectively of course. It is also possible to undergo dissociation into two, three, four parts. When the number of personality splits reaches a two-place figure, you obtain a thronging effect. At which point we are no longer dealing with an ego, but a wego. A plurality of minds in a single body. And there are *am*plifiers to intensify the inner life and give it precedence over the objective, outside world. Yes, such are the times we live in, my boy! *Omnis est Pillula!* The pharmacopoeia has become our Book of Life, our almanac, encyclopedia, the alpha and omega of our existence, with not a coup or overthrow in sight, for we have insurrectal suppositories, mutinine and dissidone, and that Dr. Hopkins of yours does a whopping business with his sodomil and gomorrephine—you can personally visit death and destruction upon as many cities as you like. Promotion to God Almighty is also possible, for a dollar seventy-five."

"The latest art form is tingling," I remarked. "I've heard, or rather felt, Kitschekov's *Scherzo*, but can't say it had any esthetic effect on me. I laughed in all the wrong places."

"Yes, that's not for the likes of us, grandfather stiffs from another century, castaways in time." Trottelreiner grew pensive. But then he shrugged it off, cleared his throat, looked me in the eye and said:

"Tichy, the Futurological Congress is convening now—to consider the hencity of the human race. This is their 76th World Assembly. Today I sat in on the first organizational meeting—preliminaries to the preliminaries—and would like to share my impressions with you . . ."

"Strange," I said. "I've been reading the papers fairly carefully and haven't seen any mention of this congress."

"It's a secret congress. Surely you understand—among other things to be discussed are problems concerning masconation!"

"Problems? Is something going wrong?"

"Terribly wrong!" exclaimed the Professor. "It couldn't be worse!"

"Yesterday you were singing a somewhat different tune," I said.

"That's true. But look at my situation—*only now* am I becoming acquainted with the actual state of affairs. And what I heard today, ach, I tell you—but here, you can swallow it for yourself."

Out of his briefcase he pulled a thick bundle of candy cane up-to-the-minute reports, tied together with multicolored ribbons, and handed it to me across the desk.

"Before you tackle these, a few words of explanation are in order. Pharmacocracy is psychemocracy founded upon absolute lubricracy—that is the motto of our new age. The reign of hallucinogens goes hand in glove with political corruption, to put it more plainly. And it is to this that we owe our universal disarmament."

"So at last I'm to learn just how that came about!" I cried.

"It's quite simple, really. Bribery serves one of two ends: either to dispose of a defective or otherwise undesirable commodity, or else to acquire a commodity of which there is a shortage. Services may of course be included under the heading of commodity. For a manufacturer, the ideal situation obviously is to receive payment without giving anything in return. I suppose the actualysis was started by the scandals of the malculators and mendacitors. You must have heard of them."

"Yes, but what is actualysis?"

"The breaking down, the eroding of reality. When the first bombshell broke about the graft, embrozzlement and cover-ups, all the blame was put on the computers. Though in fact powerful syndicates and secret cartels were involved. At stake was the terraforming, the making habitable of the planets—a vital undertaking for an overcrowded world! Enormous fleets of rockets had to be built, the climates and atmospheres of Saturn and Uranus had to be changed. How much simpler, then, to do all this on paper only!"

"But surely that sort of thing would be quickly exposed," I protested.

"Not at all. Unforeseen difficulties arise, unanticipated obstacles, snags, and new expenditures are required, supplementary allocations, additional funding. The Uranus Project, for example—980 billion dollars poured into it, and no indication that so much as a single stone was touched."

"Supervisory commissions?"

"Supervisory commissions don't have astronauts on them, and without the necessary preparation and training you can't very well go investigating other planets. So representatives were sent, plenipotentiaries, envoys, and these in turn relied entirely on the materials given them—receipts, photographs, statistics—and yet documents may be falsified, forged, or, what is easiest of all, fabricated by mascons."

"Ah!"

"Precisely. It was in much the same way, I imagine, that the simulation of weaponry began. After all, the private firms that received government contracts were out to make a profit too. They took billions and did nothing. That is, they produced the laser cannons all right, the launchers, anti-anti-anti-antiballistic missiles with sixth-generation multiple warheads, flying tanks and boring torpedoes, but it was all troped."

"Come again?"

"Psychotroped, hallucinated. Why run nuclear tests if you have fungol gum?"

"What's that?"

"You chew it and see mushroom clouds. Anyway, the whole thing snowballed. What need is there to train soldiers? In case of mobilization give them boot-camp capsules. And what's the point of cultivating officers in expensive military academies—don't we have strategine, tacticol, maneuvrium, commanderil? 'Studying Clausewitz all day is rough, Become a general with just one puff.' Ever hear that saying?"

"Never."

"No, because these drugs are classified, or at least unavailable to the general public. It's no longer necessary to call out the national guard—all you have to do is sprinkle the right mascon over the troubled area and the populace will see paratrooper units landing, marines charging, tanks—a real tank now costs about a million dollars, while a hallucinated one amounts to less than one-hundredth of a cent per person, or centispecter per spectator. A destroyer costs a dime. Today you could fit the whole arsenal of the United States inside a single truck. Caissons, cadaverons, bombons—in solids, liquids, gases. I understand they even have an entire Martian invasion—it's a specially prepared scenario powder."

"Everything in mascons?"

"Just about! By degrees the real army became superfluous. Only a few planes are left—I think. And who needs them? The process went like a chain reaction, there was no way to stop it. And that, my lad, is the whole secret behind disarmament. But disarmament is only part of it. Have you seen the new cadillacs, dodges, chevrolets?"

"Of course. They're not bad."

The Professor gave me the flask.

"Here, go to the window and take a look at your pretty cars with this."

I leaned out over the window sill. Seen from the forty-first floor, the street was a ravine, and at the bottom of it ran a glittering river of automobiles, windshields and polished tops flashing in the sun. I lifted the open bottle to my nose, blinked, wiped the tears from my eyes, and beheld a most unusual sight. Holding their hands out chest-high and gripping the air like children pretending to be drivers, businessmen were trotting single file down the middle of the street. Now and then between the close columns and rows of these gallopers, who were furiously pumping their legs and leaning back from the waist up, as if reclining in deep seats, a solitary car would appear, puffing and chugging along. Then the vapor wore off, the picture gave a shudder, straightened out, and once again I was looking down on a gleaming procession of car tops, white, yellow, emerald, moving majestically across Manhattan.

"A nightmare!" I said with disgust. "But even so, *pax orbi et urbi* has been established, so perhaps it's worth it."

"Yes, there are certain benefits. The number of coronaries has fallen dramatically, for these long-distance sprints are excellent exercise. On the other hand there's an increase in the number of people suffering from fallen arches, varicose veins, emphysema and enlargement of the heart. Not everyone is fit to run in a marathon."

"And that's why you don't have a car!" I exclaimed.

The Professor only smiled wryly.

"An ecomomy model nowadays sells for around 450 dollars," he said. "But when you consider that the production costs come to, roughly, an eighth of a cent, that price is pretty steep. The people who make something real—they're a vanishing breed. Composers accept their fees, pay their patrons kickbacks, and to the public that comes to the philharmonium to hear the commissioned work performed they slip a little polysymphonicol contrapuntaline."

"Morally that's indefensible," I said, "but surely not harmful on the social level."

"So far, no. Though in the final analysis it all depends upon your point of view. With metamorphine, for example, you can have an affair with a goat, thinking it's Venus de Milo herself. Instead of scientific papers and conventions —congressil and decongressol, and yet there must exist some biological minimum—the bare necessities of life—which no fiction can ever replace. One has to live *somewhere*, after all, eat *something*, breathe *something*. Meanwhile actualysis robs us of one sphere of genuine activity after another. Besides which we are getting a frightening accumulation of side effects. And these require the use of dehallucinides, supermascons and fixators—with dubious success."

"What are they?"

"The dehallucinides? A new series. They create the illusion that there is no illusion. At the present they're given only to the mentally ill, but the number of people who suspect the authenticity of their surroundings is growing in leaps and bounds. The amnestives can do nothing against sursurmises or doubledoubts. For these are secondary fantasies, in other words twice removed. You don't understand? Well, say someone imagines that he is only imagining that he doesn't imagine—or the other way around. A typical problem for modern psychiatry, what they call multistage paranoia. But the most ominous are the new mascons. You see, all these drugs, they take their toll on the organism. People's hair starts falling out, ears grow horny, chitinous, and tails begin to disappear again . . ."

"Appear again, you meant to say."

"No, disappear. Everyone has a tail, for thirty years now.

That was the result of orthographine. The price we had to pay for learning so quickly how to write."

"Nonsense—I was at the beach, Professor, and nobody has a tail!"

"Don't be a child. The tails are masked, of course, with anticaudalis, which in turn causes discoloration of the nails and teeth."

"Which is also masked?"

"Naturally. Mascons operate in milligram amounts, but all told an average person absorbs about one hundred and ninety kilograms in the course of a year, which is easy to understand, when you consider that it's necessary to simulate furniture, furnishings, food, drink, obedience from one's children, courtesy from officials, scientific discoveries, ownership of Rembrandts and scissors, ocean voyages, space flights, and a million other things. Were it not for the confidentiality practiced by the medical profession, it would be known that every second inhabitant of New York is spotted, has greenish bristles growing down his back, thorns on his ears, flat feet, and emphysema with an enlarged heart from constantly galloping about. All this must be concealed, and that is precisely the function of the supermascons."

"Nightmarish! Is there no hope?"

"Our congress will entertain alternative hencities. The experts are all saying that a radical change is imperative. At this moment we have before us eighteen proposals."

"To save the world?"

"You might put it that way. But why don't you take a seat and give these materials a lick? And also, well, I have a favor to ask of you. It's a delicate matter."

"I'll do what I can."

"I was counting on that. You see, I've received from a colleague of mine, a chemist, samples of two newly synthesized vigilax derivatives—up'n'at'mizers. They arrived in the morning mail, with this letter." Trottelreiner showed me the letter on his desk. "He says that my restorative, the one you've just been using, is not the genuine article. He writes, and I quote, 'The Federal Bureau of Suggestion, Division of Psychemeering (that's Psychemengineering), in order to divert the attention of the soothseers from many critical phenomena, is deliberately and maliciously supplying them with false counterhallucinatory agents containing neomascons.' "

"It doesn't make sense. The drug you gave me works, I experienced its effects myself. And anyway, what is a soothseer?"

"A position of high social standing, which a few —including myself—have the honor and privilege to hold. Soothseeing is the right to take vigilanimides—for the purpose of determining how things are *in reality*. For *someone* has to know. That's obvious, I think?"

"Yes."

"And as for the drug, my friend's guess is that it does indeed cancel out the influence of mascons of earlier vintage, mascons introduced some time ago, but doesn't stop them all—particularly not the most recent. In which case this"—the Professor held up the flask—"would be no restorative at all, but a most treacherously devised mascon, a counterfeit countermeasure, a double reagent, or in other words a wolf in sheep's clothing!"

"But *why?* If it's necessary for someone to know . . ."

"Necessary for the general welfare, for society, for all mankind, but not from the point of view of the special interests of certain politicians, corporations, even departments of the government. If things are worse than we, the soothseers, suspect, then *they* don't want us sounding the alarm, and thus this drug is made available. Much like the old trick where one would set up easily discovered hiding places for a thief—in the hopes that he'd be satisfied with his first find and not seek out the real, far more cleverly concealed treasure!"

"Yes, I think I understand. But just what do you want of me?"

"While you're acquainting yourself with these materials, take a sniff from the first vial, here, then a sniff from the second. Frankly, I haven't the courage."

"Is that all? Hand them over, then."

I took both glass tubes from the Professor, pulled up a chair and began to familiarize myself, one by one, with the abstracts of the papers submitted to the futurological congress. The first proposal envisaged a complete restructuring of attitudes, to be brought about by the introduction into the atmosphere of a thousand tons of reversol, which would effect a full 180-degree change in everyone's feelings. In the first phase, after the dispersion of the drug, comfort, abundance, delicious food, esthetic objects, elegance—all such things would overnight become despised, while crowding, poverty, ugliness and deprivation would be valued above all else. In the second phase the mascons and superneomascons would be totally removed or neutralized. Only now would the people, confronted with reality for the first time in their lives, find happiness, for they would have before them every-thing their hearts desired. One might even activate the ex-acerbands to worsen living conditions a little. But since rever-sol makes no exceptions in its inverting effect, erotic pleas-ures too would be rendered loathsome, and that would threaten mankind with extinction. Therefore once a year for 24 hours the drug's influence would be temporarily sus-pended by an appropriate antidote. On that day we would undoubtedly have a sharp rise in the number of suicides, yet this would be more than compensated for by the simultane-ously initiated increase in the birth rate.

I can't say the plan aroused my enthusiasm. The only commendable point in it was the one which said that the originator of this proposal, as a member of the soothseer class, should himself take the antidote on a permanent basis, so that neither the ubiquitous misery nor the ugliness, neither the mire nor the tedium of life could afford him any particular delight. The second proposal provided for the dis-solving of 10,000 tons of retrotemporox in the waters of the rivers and oceans. This drug reverses the flow of subjective time. Life would thus unfold in the following fashion: people would come into the world as doddering old men and take their leave of it as newborn infants. In this way, the author argued, we would be removing the main drawback in the human condition, which is for every man the prospect of inevitable aging and death. With the passage of time, then, each senior citizen grows younger and younger, gaining in strength and vigor. Upon retirement—being underage for work—he enters the blessed realm of childhood. The humaneness of the proposal derived from that natural ignorance of the mortality of all living things which is characteristic of the very young. Of course in actual fact—since this turning back of time was purely subjective—we would not be leading babies to the kindergartens, nurseries and delivery rooms, but old men. The author wasn't too clear on what ought to be done with them after that, but only observed in a general way that they might be given suitable therapy at the national euthanasium. Reading this raised the first proposal considerably in my estimation.

The third proposal was long-range and far more drastic. It advocated ectogenesis, prostheticism and universal transception. Of man only the brain would remain, beautifully encased in duraplast: a globe equipped with sockets, plugs and clasps. And powered by atomic battery—so the ingestion of nutriments, now physically superfluous, would take place only through illusion, programmed accordingly. The brain case could be connected to any number of appendages, apparatuses, machines, vehicles, etc. This prostheticization process would be spread out over two decades, with partial replacements mandatory for the first ten years, leaving all unnecessary organs at home; for example, when going to the theater one would detach one's fornication and defecation modules and hang them in the closet. Then, in the next ten years, transcepting would do away with crowds and congestion, the consequence of overpopulation. Channels of interbrain communication, whether by cable or radio, would make pointless all gatherings and get-togethers, excursions and journeys to attend conferences, and therefore all personal locomotion to whatever location, for every living being could avail itself of sensors and scanners situated over the whole expanse of human habitation, even to the farthermost planets. Mass production would keep the market supplied with custom-made internal components and accessories, including braintracks for home railways, that would enable the heads themselves to roll from room to room, an innocent diversion. At this point I stopped and remarked that the authors of these papers were surely deranged. Trottelreiner replied coldly that I was a bit hasty in my judgments. We made our bed and now we must lie in it. Anyhow, the criterion of common sense was never applicable to the history of the human race. Averroës, Kant, Socrates, Newton, Voltaire, could any of them have believed it possible that in the twentieth century the scourge of cities, the poisoner of lungs, the mass murderer and idol of millions would be a metal receptacle on wheels, and that people would actually prefer being crushed to death inside it during frantic weekend exoduses instead of staying, safe and sound, at home? I asked him which of the proposals he intended to support.

"I haven't yet decided," he said. "The gravest problem, in my opinion, is the increase in underground natalities—you know, unlicensed births. And besides that, I'm afraid there may be some psychem tampering in the course of the deliberations."

"How do you mean?"

"A proposal could be passed with the help of a gullibloon or two."

"You think they'd actually try such a thing?"

"Why not? What could be easier than pumping gas into our conference hall through the air conditioning?"

"But whatever the congress endorses doesn't have to be

accepted by the public. The people won't take everything lying down."

"Come now, Tichy. For half a century civilization hasn't been left to its own devices. A hundred years ago a certain Dior was dictating fashions in clothing. Today this sort of regulating has embraced all walks of life. If prostheticism is voted in, I assure you, in a couple of years everyone will consider the possession of a soft, hairy, sweating body to be shameful and indecent. A body needs washing, deodorizing, caring for, and even then it breaks down, while in a prostheticized society you can snap on the loveliest creations of modern engineering. What woman doesn't want to have silver iodide instead of eyes, telescopic breasts, angel's wings, iridescent legs, and feet that sing with every step?"

"Listen," I said, "let's run away. We can get a supply of oxygen, provisions, and hole up somewhere in the Rocky Mountains. Remember the sewers of the Hilton? It wasn't all that bad there, was it?"

"You're not serious?" began the Professor, as if hesitating.

By sheer accident I happened to raise the vial to my nose—I had completely forgotten that I was still holding it. Tears welled up from the acrid smell. I sneezed, and sneezed again, and when I opened my eyes the room had changed. The Professor was still speaking, I could hear his voice but, fascinated by the transformation, no longer listened to the words. The walls were now all covered with grime; the blue sky had taken on a brownish tinge; some of the windowpanes were missing, and the rest had a coat of greasy soot, streaked with gray from previous rains.

I don't know why, but it was particularly upsetting to see

that the Professor's handsome briefcase, the one in which he'd brought the conference materials, had turned into a moldy old satchel. I grew numb. I was afraid to look at him. I peeked under the desk. Instead of his appliquéd trousers and professorial spats there were two casually crossed artificial legs. Between the wire tendons of the feet bits of gravel were lodged, and mud from the street. The steel pin of the heel gleamed, worn smooth with use. I groaned.

"What is it, a headache? Want an aspirin?" came the sympathetic voice. I gritted my teeth and looked up.

Not much was left of the face. Stuck to his sunken cheeks were the rotting shreds of a bandage that hadn't been changed in ages. And evidently he still wore glasses, though one of the lenses was cracked. In his neck, in the opening of a tracheotomy, a vocoder had been inserted—carelessly enough—and it bobbed up and down as he talked. A jacket hung in mildewed tatters on the rack that was his chest, and beneath the left lapel there was a gaping hole lidded with a cloudy plastic window. Inside, a heart, held together with clamps and staples, beat in blue-black spasms. I didn't see a left hand; the right, clutching a pencil, was fashioned out of brass and green with verdigris. Sewn to his collar—a crooked label, on which someone had scribbled in red ink: "Barbr 119-859-21 transpl. /5 rejec." I stared, eyes popping, while the Professor, taking on my horror like a mirror, suddenly froze behind his desk.

"I . . . I've changed, haven't I?" he croaked.

The next thing I knew, I was struggling with the doorknob.

"Tichy! What are you doing? Come back! Tichy!!" he cried in despair, struggling to stand up. The door swung open, but just then I heard an awful clatter. Professor Trottelreiner, losing his balance from an overly violent movement, had toppled over and fallen apart on the floor, hooks and hinges snapping like bones. I carried away with me the image of his helpless kicking, the flailing iron stumps that sent chips of wood flying, the dark sack of the heart pounding desperately behind the scratched plastic. Down the corridor I ran, as if driven by a hundred Furies.

The building swarmed with people, I had hit on the lunch hour. Out of the offices came clerks and secretaries, chatting as they headed for the elevators. I elbowed my way through the crowd towards one of the open doors, but apparently the elevator car hadn't yet arrived; looking into the empty shaft, I immediately understood why panting was so common a phenomenon. The end of the cable, long since disconnected, was hanging loose, and the people were clambering, agile as monkeys, up the vertical cage that enclosed the shaft—they must have had a lot of practice. Crawling up to the snack bar on the roof, they conversed cheerfully despite the sweat dripping from their brows. I backed off slowly, then ran down the stairway that spiraled around the shaft with the climbers patiently scaling its sides. A few flights lower I slowed down. They were still pouring out of all the doors. Nothing but offices here, evidently. At the end of the hall shone an open window, looking out on the street. I stopped by it, pretending to straighten my tie, and peered down. At first it seemed to me that there wasn't a living soul in that crowd on the sidewalk, but I simply hadn't recognized the pedestrians. The general splendor had disappeared without a trace. They walked separately, in pairs, clothed in rags

—patches, holes—many with bandages and plasters, some in only their underwear, which enabled me to verify that they were indeed spotted and had bristles, mainly on their backs. A few had evidently been released from the hospital to attend to some urgent business; amputees and paraplegics rolled along on boards with little wheels, talking and laughing loudly. I saw women with drooping elephant flaps for ears, men with horns on their heads, old newspapers, clumps of straw or burlap bags carried with the utmost elegance and aplomb. Those who were healthier and in better condition raced on the road, cantering, prancing, kicking up their feet as if changing gears. Robots predominated in the crowd, wielding atomizers, dosimeters, spray guns, sprinklers. Their job was to see that everyone got his share of aerosol. Nor did they limit themselves to that: behind one young couple, arms around each other—hers were covered with scales, his with boils—there plodded an old clonker, methodically beating the lovers over the head with a watering can. Their teeth rattled, but they were perfectly oblivious. Was it doing this on purpose? I could no longer think. Gripping the window sill, I stared at the scene in the street, its bustle, its rush, its industry, as if I were the only witness, the only pair of eyes. The only? No, the cruelty of this spectacle demanded at least another observer, its creator, the one who, without intervening in that grim panorama, would give it meaning; a patron, an impresario of decay, therefore a ghoul—but someone. A tiny juggermugger, cavorting around the legs of a spry old lady, repeatedly undercut her knees, and she fell flat on her face, got up, walked on, was tripped again, and so they went, it mechanically persistent, she energetic and determined, until they were out of sight. Many of the robots hovered over the people, peering into their mouths, possibly to check the effect of the sprays, though it didn't exactly look that way. On the corner stood a bunch of robots, loiterants, dejects; out of some side alley came shifts of drudgers, kludgers, meniacs and manikoids; an enormous trashmaster rumbled along the curb, lifting up on the claws of its shovel whatever lay in the way, tossing—together with junkets and selfaborts—an old woman into its disposal bin. I bit my knuckles, forgetting that that hand held the other vial, the second vial, and my throat was seared with fire. Everything wavered, a bright fog descended across my eyes like a blindfold, which an unseen hand then slowly began to lift. I looked, petrified, at the transformation taking place, realizing in a sudden shudder of premonition that now reality was sloughing off yet another layer—clearly, its falsification had begun so very long ago, that even the most powerful antidote could do no more than tear away successive veils, reaching the veils beneath but not the truth. It grew brighter—white. Snow lay on the pavement, frozen solid, trampled down by hundreds of feet; the street presented a bleak and colorless scene; the shops, the signs had vanished, and instead of glass in the windows —rotting boards, crossed and nailed together. Winter reigned between the dingy, discolored buildings, long icicles hung from the lintels, lamps; in the sharp air there was a sour smell, and a bluish gray haze, like the sky above. Mounds of dirty snow along the walls, garbage heaped in the gutters; here and there a shapeless bundle, a dark clump of rags kicked to the side by the constant stream of pedestrian traffic, or shoved between rusty trashcans, tins, boxes, frozen sawdust. Snow wasn't falling at the moment, but one could see that it had fallen recently, and would again. Then all at once I knew what was missing: the robots. There wasn't a single robot on the street—not one! Their snow-covered bodies lay sprawled in doorways, lifeless iron hulks in the company of human refuse, scraps of clothing, with an occasional bone showing underneath, yellow, sheathed with ice. One ragamuffin sat atop a pile of snow, settling down for the night as if in a feather bed; I saw the contentment on his face; he felt right at home, apparently, made himself comfortable, stretched his legs, wriggled his naked toes into the snow. So that was that chill, that strange invigoration which came over one from time to time, even in the middle of the street, at noon, with the sun shining—he was already snoring peacefully—so *that* was the reason. The throngs of people passing by ignored him, they were occupied with themselves—some were spraying others. It was easy to tell from their manner who thought himself a human, and who a robot. So the robots too were only a fiction? And what was winter doing here in the middle of summer? Unless the whole calendar was a hoax. But why? Sleeping in snow to lower the birth rate? Whichever, someone had carefully planned it all and I wasn't about to give up the ghost before I tracked him down. I lifted my eyes to the skyscrapers, their pock-marked sides and rows of broken windows. It was quiet behind me: lunch was over. The street—the street was all that was left to me now, my new-found sight would be to no advantage there, I would be swallowed up in that crowd, and I needed someone; alone, I'd hide for a time like a rat—that was the most I could do—no longer safely inside the illusion, but shipwrecked in reality. Horrified, despairing, I backed away from the window, chilled to the bone, unprotected now by the lie of a temperate climate. I didn't know myself where I was going, trying to make as little noise as possible; yes, I was already concealing my presence—crouching, skulking, furtively glancing over my shoulder, halting, listening—a creature of reflex, making no decisions, though I was certain that the fact that I could see was plainly written on my face and I would have to pay for it. I went down the corridor, it was either the sixth or fifth floor, I couldn't go back to Trottelreiner—he needed help, but I had none to give him—I was thinking feverishly about several things at once, but mainly about whether or not the drug would wear off and I would find myself back in Paradise. Strange, but the prospect filled me with nothing but fear and loathing, as if I would have rather shivered in some garbage dump—with the knowledge that that was what it was—than owed my deliverance to apparitions. My way down a side passage was blocked by an old man; too feeble to walk, he gave an imitation of it with his trembling legs, and managed a smile of greeting even as he breathed his last, the death rattle already in his throat. So I went another way—till I reached the frosted glass of some office. Complete silence inside. I entered through the swinging door and saw a hall with rows of typewriters—empty. At the other end, another door, half-open. I could see into the large, bright room, and began to retreat, for someone was there, but a familiar voice rang out:

"Come in, Tichy."

So I went in. I wasn't even that surprised that he'd been waiting for me, and I took it calmly, too, that there on the other side of the desk sat George P. Symington Esquire himself, in a gray flannel suit, a natty ascot around his neck and a thin cigarillo in his mouth. And wearing sunglasses. He seemed to look at me with either amusement or regret, I couldn't tell which.

"Have a seat," he said, "this will take a while."

I sat. The room, with windowpanes intact, was an oasis of tidiness and warmth in the general neglect: no freezing drafts, no snowdrifts in the corners, a pot of steaming black coffee, an ashtray, a dictaphone, and hanging on the wall above his head—a few female nudes, in color. Odd, though, that those photographed bodies should have no scales or bristles. And odd, that that should strike me odd.

"Now you've done it!" he said abruptly. "And note that you have only yourself to blame! The best nurse, the only soothseer in the neighborhood, everyone doing his best to help you, but no, you had to go rooting around for the 'truth' on your own!"

"Me?" I said, stunned by his words, and before I could gather my thoughts, before I could digest what he was saying, he snapped:

"Please, no lies. It's a little late for that. You thought you were being so frightfully clever, parading out all those protests, those grievances of yours, those suspicions about 'hallucinating'—'sewers,' 'hotel rats,' 'mounting,' 'saddling.' And did you really think such primitive inventions would serve the purpose? Only a grandfather stiff could be so incredibly stupid!"

I listened to him, my mouth hanging open. Then suddenly it hit me—any denial would be in vain, he would never believe me. For he took my genuine obsessions for some sort of maneuver! In other words, that previous conversation in which he'd revealed to me the secrets of Procrustics, Inc., it was only to draw me out, that was why he'd used those words which threw me into such confusion at the time. Perhaps he thought that they were passwords—for initiation into some antipsychem conspiracy? My private fear of hallucination he read as a tactical move, a gambit . . . Yes, it was indeed too late for explanations, particularly now that the cards were on the table.

"You were waiting for me here?" I asked.

"Of course. With all your initiative and enterprise we were in full control throughout. No unmonitored rebellion can be permitted to threaten the status quo."

The old man dying in the corridor—it dawned on me—he too had been a part of the system of barriers that led me here . . .

"A nice status quo," I said. "And you're in charge, I suppose? Congratulations."

"Save your sarcasm for a more suitable occasion!" he hissed. I had succeeded in touching on a sore point. He was annoyed.

"All this time you've been looking for some 'diabolical plot.' Well, let me tell you, my fine feathered defrostee, let me satisfy your curiosity here and now—there's no such thing. It doesn't exist. Do you understand? We keep this civilization narcotized, for otherwise it could not endure itself. That is why its sleep must not be disturbed. And that is why you will be returned to it. Oh there's nothing to fear —for you, this will be not only painless, but pleasurable.

Our lot is far more difficult; we must remain awake, to watch over you."

"A noble sacrifice," I said. "For the common good, no doubt."

"If you value your almighty freedom of thought," he said coldly, "then I would advise you to drop these snide remarks, for you'll only have to part with it that much sooner."

"Very well then. You have something else to tell me? I'm listening."

"At this moment I am the only man in the whole state, besides yourself, who can see! What am I wearing on my face?" he suddenly asked, as if to trap me.

"Sunglasses."

"Then you see as well as I!" he said. "The chemist who provided Trottelreiner with those antidotes has returned to the bosom of society and no longer harbors the least suspicion. No one must suspect. Surely you can understand that."

"Wait a minute," I said. "It really matters to you, doesn't it, that I be convinced? But—but why?"

"Soothseers aren't monsters!" he answered. "We are prisoners of the situation, backed into a corner, forced to play out the hand that history has dealt us. We bring peace and contentment in the only way remaining. We hold in precarious balance that which without us would plunge into the throes of universal agony. We are the last Atlas of this world. And if it must perish, let it at least not suffer. If the truth cannot be altered, let us at least conceal it. This is the *last* humanitarian act, the *last* moral obligation."

"Then nothing can be done? Nothing at all?" I asked.

"The year is 2098," he said, "with 69 billion inhabitants legally registered and approximately another 26 billion in hiding. The average annual temperature has fallen four degrees. In fifteen or twenty years there will be glaciers here. We have no way of averting or halting their advance—we can only keep them secret."

"I always thought there would be ice in hell," I said. "And so you paint the gates with pretty pictures?"

"Exactly," he said. "We are the last Samaritans. Someone had to speak to you from this place—it happens that I am that man."

"Yes, I seem to recall: *ecce homo!*" I said. "But wait . . . now I see what it is you're after. You want to make a believer of me, you want me to accept your role of—of eschatological anesthetist. When there's no bread—let them eat opium! But I don't understand why you're so bent on my conversion, which in any event I'm to forget completely. If the methods you employ are good, then what's the point of all this reasoning and argument? A few drops of credendium, a single squirt in the eyes, and I applaud your every word with enthusiasm, you have my full approval, my esteem. *If* those methods are good. Yet apparently you yourself are not convinced of their worth, preferring simple, old-fashioned hot air and rhetoric, wasting words on me instead of reaching for the atomizer! Apparently you're well aware that the triumph of psychem is a sham, and that you will be standing on the field alone, a conqueror with a bad case of heartburn. Yes, you wanted to win me over, then cast me off into oblivion, but it won't work. I say to hang with your lofty mission, and those whores on the wall who soften the burden of your saviorhood. You like them the good old way, I take it, without bristles?"

His face was twisted with rage. He jumped up, shouting:

"I have other drugs besides the heavenly delights! There are also chemical infernos!"

I stood up too. He was reaching for the button on his desk when I cried, "We'll go together!"—and leaped for his throat. The momentum carried us—as I had planned—to the open window. Then there were footsteps and iron hands trying to pull me from him, while he writhed and kicked, but we were on the sill now, I was pushing him, bending him back, gathering the last of my strength, leaping; the air whistled in our ears, we went head over heels, still grappling, the spinning funnel of the street rushed up—I readied myself for a bone-crushing blow but the impact, when it came, was soft, black waves surging up and the stinking, blessed waters closing over my head, then opening again. I surfaced in the middle of the sewer, wiping my eyes, gulping, choking on the foul swill but happy, happy! Professor Trottelreiner, roused from his slumber by my ungodly howls, leaned out over the edge of the platform and offered me—like a brotherly hand—the handle of his tightly wound umbrella. The thunder of the LTN bombs was dying down. The Hilton managers were all spread out in a row on their inflatable reclining chairs (inflatable-inflagrantable, the concuballoons!), and the secretaries were carrying on most provocatively in their sleep. Jim Stantor, snoring, turned over on his side and nearly smothered a rat that was nibbling at the chocolate in his pocket—both were frightened. Meanwhile

Professor Dringenbaum, that methodical Swiss, was squatting next to the wall and by the yellowish glow of the flashlight making corrections in his paper with a fountain pen. Then it occurred to me that this intense activity of his was heralding the beginning of the second day of deliberations of the Futurological Congress, and I burst into such violent laughter, that the manuscript slipped from his hands, hit the dark water with a splash, and floated away—off into the unknown future.

# BEFORE THE GOLDEN AGE 1

## Isaac Asimov

For many s.f. addicts the Golden Age began in 1938 when John Campbell became editor of Astounding Stories. For Isaac Asimov, the formative and most memorable period came in the decade before the Golden Age – the 1930s. It is to the writers of this generation that BEFORE THE GOLDEN AGE is dedicated.

Some – Jack Williamson, Murray Leinster, Stanley Weinbaum and Asimov himself – have remained famous to this day. Others such as Neil Jones, S. P. Meek and Charles Tanner, have been deservedly rescued from oblivion.

BEFORE THE GOLDEN AGE was originally published in the United States in a single mammoth volume of almost 1,200 pages. The British paperback edition will appear in four books, the first of which covers the years 1930 to 1933.

# BEFORE THE GOLDEN AGE 3

## Isaac Asimov

In this third volume, Isaac Asimov has selected a feast of rousing tales such as BORN BY THE SUN by Jack Williamson, with its marvellous vision of the solar system as a giant incubator; Murray Leinster's story of parallel time-tracks SIDEWISE IN TIME; and Raymond Z. Gallin's OLD FAITHFUL which features one of science fiction's most memorable aliens – Number 774.

'Sheer nostalgic delight . . . stories by authors long-forgotten mingle with those by ones who are well-known, and still writing. A goldmine for anyone interested in the evolution of s.f.'
*Sunday Times*

'Contains some of the very best s.f. from the Thirties . . . emphatically value for money.'
*Evening Standard*

# A MIDSUMMER TEMPEST

## Poul Anderson

'The best writing he's done in years ... his language is superb. Worth buying for your permanent collection.'
– *The Alien Critic*

Somewhere, spinning through another universe, is an Earth where a twist of fate, a revolution and a few early inventions have made a world quite unlike our own.

It is a world where Cavaliers and Puritans battle with the aid of observation balloons and steam trains; where Oberon and Titania join forces with King Arthur to resist the Industrial Revolution; and where the future meshes with the past in the shape of Valeria, time traveller from New York.

# THE FOREVER WAR

## Joe Haldeman

Winner of the 1976 Nebula and Hugo Awards.

Earth has been fighting for its life against an alien civilization which simply will not negotiate.

The elite of Earth's young people are trained to fight a war fought at speeds approaching that of light. Relativity comes into play. A group of young people will leave the Earth aged 27 and return *two of their years later* to find that the Earth and the war have moved on by fifty, a hundred, maybe several hundred years.

Making brilliant use of this paradox and the wellnigh impossible logistics of fighting such a war, Joe Haldeman has given us the most impressive SF novel of the past ten years—an instant classic.

# THE MOTE IN GOD'S EYE

## Larry Niven and Jerry Pournelle

An alien space ship, using some motive power unknown to man comes sailing into the outer reaches of the solar system.

The team sent to intercept it accidentally destroy it, but its course has been recorded accurately enough to extrapolate its point of origin.

A team of scientists, escorted by the most powerful battleship in Earth's space fleet is sent to contact this newly discovered civilization. What they find is at once the most exciting and tragic destiny ever to be suffered by sentient beings.

'The best novel about human beings making first contact with intelligent but utterly nonhuman aliens I have ever seen, and possibly the finest science fiction novel I have ever read.'—Robert A. Heinlein.

'A spellbinder, a swashbuckler . . . and best of all a brilliant new approach to that fascinating problem—first contact with aliens.'—Frank Herbert.